DEDICATED TO MY WIFE

ISBN: 978-1-907179-73-0

A CIP catalogue for this book is available from the
National Library.

Published by ORIGINAL WRITING LTD., Dublin, 2010.

Printed by CAHILL PRINTERS LIMITED, Dublin.

COUNTRY BOYS

by

J.P. Diamond

ORIGINAL WRITING

Synopsis

This short novel describes the lives of several teenagers from a Working-class Irish Catholic background, growing up in rural Northern Ireland during an eleven-month period in the early 1970's. The strong family ties, work ethic and sense of humour are recurring themes in the book, but the omnipresent threat of the "Troubles" lurks menacingly in the background.

CHAPTER 1

Friday 14th July 1972.

It was a warm summers evening. Sean Daly and his cousin
Patsy had just finished loading a trailer of bales of hay for
his Uncle Gerry, Patsy's daddy. The load had been built five
bales high; Gerry didn't like to build too high as he had done so
a couple of years ago, only for the load to come off on the way
home. This year he was going to play safe - farming a small plot
of land in Northern Ireland was hard enough without making
life harder for yourself. Besides - the forecast was good for the
next few days and they weren't in any hurry. Uncle Gerry was
driving the tractor, a red Massey Ferguson which he had bought
secondhand back in the late 1960's, and Sean and Patsy were sitting perched up on top of the load as they made their way slowly
back to the hayshed a couple or three miles down the road in the
townland of Urrismore, about three miles outside Lamagh, in Co
Tyrone. There was a cool breeze blowing now. The faraway ring-
ing of the Angelus bell in the local chapel signified that it had just
turned 6 o'clock - and it gave an almost soothing relief as they
had been working since mid-morning under the warm July sun.
For Sean, this was his favourite part of the day; chewing a piece
of newly mown hay and looking up at the clear blue sky. His days
work was nearly done and soon he would be having a warm bath
and getting his tea. Sean's father Peter worked for the Electricity

Board and wasn't with them tonight but he'd be off tomorrow. Sean always liked it when his daddy was with them but he had to be careful with his language as his da was very holy and didn't like cursing. Sometimes, when you were lifting bales, you could get a jag on your finger or worse, under the fingernail; and Sean found it therapeutic on such occasions to let off steam with a few four-letter words. That tendency had to be curtailed when Peter was with them.

Sean and Patsy were more like brothers than cousins. They were both thirteen years of age, had grown up together and were in the same class through primary school. Occasionally they would fight and disagree, but disagreements never lasted long and anyone picking a fight with either of them in the schoolyard soon found themselves confronted with two opponents rather than one. Sean was taller than Patsy but of finer build. Patsy was a faster runner than Sean over short distances but Sean would have had the edge over the longer distances. Currently they both played for the local Under-14 Gaelic team, Tir-Na-Nog, though they would shortly be graduating to the Under-16's. Patsy was just over six weeks younger than Sean. Sean thought his cousin was the best player on the team and might even play for Tyrone one day. As far as his own football skills were concerned, Sean reckoned that, competent trier though he was, his true vocation in life lay somewhere other than on the football field.

As they negotiated the final bend, just before taking the turn-off into the laneway leading into the farmyard, Patsy remarked, "you know somethin' Sean – I'm glad you and me live out here even though we have to work all day in the heat. I'd hate to be stuck in a housin' estate like Kevin and those boys in weather like this." "I know what you mean," said Sean. "Kevin's probably sittin' on his ars this evenin' in watchin' the TV or somethin." Kevin was a classmate of theirs who lived in Lamagh town. He was also on their under –14 team, though he was a better soccer player than he was at the Gaelic. Soccer was the main pastime of Kevin and his mates on the estate, though in the last year Kevin had discovered a new pastime which he found was even more fun than soccer - girls.

The entrance to the hayshed was quite narrow and Gerry had little space to manoeuvre as he reversed the tractor, slowly edging the load as near as he could to where the rest of the bales had been built. If they were building high up he would have used the elevator, but it wouldn't be needed this evening. When the trailer had nearly stopped, Patsy jumped off and unloosened the knot which his da had tied. God knows how his da had learned that knot, but Patsy would get him to show it to him someday. Thankfully it wasn't as hot inside the hayshed now as it had been earlier. Knowing that this was the last load of the day made Patsy and Sean work twice as hard to get the load off as quickly as possible. Gerry had gone off to make a phone call to a neighbour of his who owned a baler. There was still another field to bale and Gerry reckoned that the rain wouldn't hold out for much longer. Sean threw the bales down to Patsy who put them in neat, tight rows. Before long the trailer had been emptied and the pair of them proceeded towards the kitchen where Gerry's wife Kathleen had been busy making their tea. Sean, who had a healthy appetite, always looked forward to eating tea at his Aunt Kathleen's house, mainly because of her delicious home-made rhubarb tart which was always fresh and hot out of the oven. As they headed to the bathroom to wash their hands and face, Sean inhaled the sweet aroma which permeated the small house. They sat down to the table and his aunt set down a plate of roast beef sandwiches. Gerry arrived in, having made his phone call, and took his seat at the top of the table. Sean was thirsty and poured himself a large glass of orange quosh which had been cooled with ice-cubes. It had been over 20deg. C. for a good part of the day and he savoured the cool liquid as it disappeared down his throat. "Barney said that he'll be able to come tomorrow mornin' at half-eleven. You boys make sure you don't have any other plans," instructed Gerry, before proceeding to take a large bite out of one of the sandwiches. "Can we get Kevin to come over?" inquired Patsy of his father. "If you want," replied Gerry. "The more help the better." "I'll ring him tonight," answered Patsy. "Do you want any more tea Sean?" asked Kathleen. "No thanks Aunt Kathleen." His aunt then lifted the tart out of the stove. She proceeded to cut three large pieces and put one on each plate. She had also prepared some whipped cream and put a large spoonful on top of each piece. She handed a plate to each of them. Sean savoured the taste of the hot, tangy tart mixed with the cool whipped cream as the first piece entered his mouth. All the sweating and hard work was worth it to have this as your end-of-day reward. He took his time eating it and was in no hurry to finish.

"Kathleen, could ye turn that radio on at Ulster – the forecast will be comin'on after the news," mentioned Gerry to his wife. Kathleen turned on the radio and the news had just started. "Six people were killed in separate incidents across Northern Ireland last night. Three of the dead were British Army soldiers who died when their landrover was blown up near Crossmaglen in South Armagh. In Belfast, two men were blown up in a house off the Falls area of the city. It's thought they may have been handling the device when it exploded. The body of another man has been found in an alleyway in the east of the city. He had been shot in the head." "What's this country going to be like another couple of years from now?" exclaimed Gerry. "People are being killed every day now." "The two boys who blew themselves up must have been IRA men," noted Patsy. Sean got the impression that Patsy had a twinge of sympathy for The IRA men. One thing was sure – neither of them had any sympathy for the dead British Army soldiers. Back in January that year, the British Army paratroopers had shot dead thirteen people after a Civil Rights march in Derry city. Sean, who, at thirteen years of age, did not find politics terribly interesting, was shocked when he saw it on the news. Occasionally their car would be stopped by British soldiers and Sean was always wary of them. His father Peter was always polite with them at the checkpoints, but never to the point of friendliness. He heard his father say once to his mother Brigid that he didn't mind the British as much as the U.D.R., who were just a bunch of Protestant bigots, no better than their predecessors, the B-Specials.

"The weather forecast for the next few days will be dry and cloudy – temperatures will vary between 18 and 22deg. Celsius. Next news at nine pm." "Dry 'n cloudy will do all-right," said Gerry as he finished off the last piece of tart. "Are ye goin' into the bingo tonight Kathleen?" 'No – I'll give it a miss Gerry – besides you might need me tomorrow, so I'm going to get an early night tonight. Don't forget to take your bath later Patsy." "Will do ma," promised Patsy. "Sean – ye must be tired son. Do ye want a lift up the road before I go for me bath?" "Wouldn't mind Uncle Gerry." The three of them climbed into Gerry's white Hillman Hunter to leave Sean home. Sean lived in the "home place" where the Daly family had been reared. His Granda, who was seventy-eight, lived with him, his two sisters and his father and mother. When Gerry had got married he had built a house on a patch of the Daly land about half a mile from where he had been brought up. His granny had died back in the early 60's. Peter and Gerry had another two sisters and brothers but they were all married and living elsewhere. It was pretty hard to get work in this part of Northern Ireland, especially if you were a Catholic. They made their way up the narrow road. About a hundred yards ahead of them was an Army landrover. Three or four soldiers were stopping cars. Gerry took his place in the middle of the three-car queue. The car in front was waved on. Sean recognised the car. It belonged to Robert Smith – a local Protestant farmer. Gerry rolled down his window. A soldier with a blackened face peered in at the occupants and asked, "'ave yuh got ya Droiving Licence on ya Sih?" What a strange accent, thought Sean. This man speaks the same language as I do - it's like he's speaking English, but with a foreign accent. "I have – yeah," retorted Gerry, producing the blue, dog-eared driving licence from the glove compartment. "Where are you off to then?" "I'm leavin' my nephew home." "And where would that be?"" That house there," said Gerry, pointing his finger at Sean's house which was no more than 50 yards from where they had been stopped. "OK suh," said the soldier – handing back the driving licence.They continued on their way. "I wonder how much those boys get paid for doin' that?" wondered Patsy. "Like - I've spent the day doin' somethin' useful and I haven't got paid anything." "Your reward will be great in heaven my lad," chuckled Gerry to his son.

As Sean got out of the car, Peter, who had just arrived home himself, came out to meet them. Peter was two years younger than Gerry. He had just turned forty-nine. They were physically similar, Peter being slightly taller than his brother at 5'10". "Ye got on O.K. today," said Peter. "Aye – we got that wee field red up. We'll be gettin' the big field baled 'tomorra, all being well," replied Gerry. "That'll suit all-right as long as the rain stays away." "Aye - well the forecast gives it good. Right – I'll head on here – see ye tomorra." Peter and Sean went on into the house. Sean's mother greeted him."I just put some tea on for your father Sean – do you want some?" "No ma – I'm goin' to hop into the bath." When the bath was filling, Sean took off his tee-shirt, jeans and pants. He tested the water temperature with his toes to make sure it wasn't too hot or too cold. When the bath was full enough, he turned off the tap and lay down in the warm, luxurious water, rubbing his body with soap. His thin, wiry forearms were a reddish-brown colour. He clenched his fists and felt a power which had not been there before the haymaking had started. The hard work made him feel tough and fit, despite the fact that during the heat of the early afternoon there were times when he would much have preferred to have been resting in the shade with a cool drink. He would never have said that however, as it would not have been the manly thing to do. He put his head under the water and then poured some shampoo into his hand which he then rubbed vigorously into his fair-coloured hair. His hair was getting a little longer, but not as long as he would have liked it as his da and granda both detested long hair and would nag at him to get it cut once it reached collar level. "You'll be callin' yerself Shauna and headin' into Lamagh with a handbag next," his Granda would say. His face was warm and red as he had picked up a lot of sun today. He would try and remember and put some cream on it tomorrow. He stretched out in the bath and let all the tension which he had accumulated during the course of the day ebb from his body. Fifteen minutes later, when the water temperature had cooled somewhat he got out and scrubbed himself with the towel his mother had left for him. He put on a fresh set of clothes and went up to the sitting-room. His father was sitting in his chair reading the Irish News and his granda was in the corner smoking his pipe.

"Whereabouts were ye today da?" asked Sean. "I was up by Carrickcrudden today Sean," replied his father. "Somebody had crashed into a pole." "Is there anything on on the TV tonight," inquired Sean. Peter turned to the page where the TV listings were. "Nothin' much on tonight. One of the boys at work said that there's a documentary on tomorra' tonight about Muhammad Ali or Cassius Clay as he used to be called. He's fightin' in Croke Park next week." Sean, who was a big Ali fan, was looking forward to the fight even though the result would be a foregone conclusion. Ali didn't come to Ireland to get beaten up by an unknown in Croke Park. His Granda wasn't just as enamoured of Ali as he was. "That's that yankee boxer who's always rappin' on about how pretty he is. Imagine standin' in front of a TV camera and tellin' everybody you're so great and so pretty." "You're just jealous 'cos you've never got the chance Granda," said Brigid who had overheard the conversation and was laughing. "Actually – he is quite pretty," she added. "Even prettier than me?" said Peter, who gave his wife a tickle as he pulled her down beside him onto the armchair. Well – even if he is, he shouldn't be goin' on about it," responded Granda. "Were you anyway pretty at one time Granda?" inquired Sean. Peter and Brigid were both amused by Sean's question. Pretty wasn't really the word Sean– but I did set the odd heart a flutterin' at the ceilidhs years ago." "How did ye manage to do that?" asked his grandson. "He had that certain 'je-ne-sais-qua' quality about him," interjected Brigid. Sean, who had been studying French at school, knew what 'je-ne-sais-qua' meant but he wasn't sure how it applied to his Granda. "Which did ye discover first – Mammy or the pipe?" asked Peter, referring to the two great loves of his father's life. "Oh, yer mammy came first Peter. I took up the pipe in me 40's". "You were enterin' a more reflective period of your life then." "Maybe – who's that Ali fella fightin' in Dublin next week?" "He's fightin' a boxer called Al Blue Lewis", said Sean. "Can't say I ever heard of him," replied his Granda. "If he's related to Joe Louis, he might be all right though." "Who was Joe Louis Granda," inquired Sean. "He fought about thirty years ago and he was the greatest fighter who ever lived," said his Granda. "He would have beat the lugs off that pretty boy if he'd a been around today." "Would ye mind if I beat you in a game of draughts, Granda?" "That game last week was a fluke Sean- go and get the board." Sean lifted the draught-set down from the high shelf and dragged the coffee-table over to where his Granda was sitting. He set the board out and gave his Granda the black draughts while he set out his white. About an hour later the game had ended in a stalemate. "Sean – get yourself an early night son – we'll be busy tomorra'." "OK da – night ma. Night granda." "Night Sean," his mother and Granda said in unison as he left the room.. "I doubt the days of me givin' Sean a lesson in draughts are nearly over," observed Granda. "He picks up things pretty quickly,"said Peter. "I don't know what he'll do with himself when he leaves school." "He's pretty good at science but his French and Irish results weren't too good on his last report," retorted Brigid. "As long as he's got a bit of common sense, I wouldn't be too worried if he ever learns to gabble in French or Irish for that matter," said his Granda "I better go and collect the girls from the disco," mentioned Peter. "I'll have your supper ready for you all when you come in," replied Brigid.

CHAPTER 2

Saturday 15th July 1972.

Sean was awake at 8.30am. He hadn't realised how tired he was until he had got to bed, and had slept like a log all night. He was glad that he had as today would be a busy day. They were baling the "big field" as it was known in the Daly household. At least there would be plenty of help. His daddy would be there and Kevin would be coming out from the town on his bike to give them a hand. Sean, Patsy and Kevin liked to work together as the craic between them was always good and Patsy and Kevin had plenty to say for themselves, especially on matters like school, teachers, convent girls and football. He put on his jeans and tee-shirt and made his way to the bathroom. When he got to the kitchen his mother had his breakfast ready for him. He took his piece of orange and savoured the taste of the hot porridge. He then poured himself a cup of tea and helped himself to a couple of pieces of melted cheese-on-toast.It would be the last food he would be tasting until the mid-afternoon. His father came in as Sean was finishing. "What time is the baler-man comin' at da?"inquired Sean. "Gerry rang last night and said he should be here about eleven. Do ye want to walk down to the field or come down in the car with me?" "I'll dander down meself and call in for Patsy on the way past."

It was another glorious summer morning. Sean felt good to be alive as he made his way up the short lane onto the road. The birds were singing and he could hear the distinctive call of the corncrake. It reminded him of a line in a poetry book he had at school about a nightingale which,"singest of summer in full-throated ease." Although they hadn't actually studied that particular poem yet, Sean liked to read some of the poems in the book to see if he could make sense of any of them. He particularly liked that one about the nightingale – it was called Ode to a Nightingale by John Keats. He remembered the poet's surname because it was similar to that of WB.Yeats – Ireland's most famous poet. Although there was a lot of "thee" and "thou" and words like "dryad" which he didn't understand, he liked the way the poet described things. He didn't discuss poetry with Kevin or Patsy though – that would have been an invitation to be on the receiving end of a slagging. He loved the smell of the wild flowers – if only every Saturday morning were as perfect as this. As he made his way down his Uncle Gerry's lane, he could see that Patsy was already up and about, helping his father to finish off the milking. They greeted one another. "Da, Sean and me 'll take the tractor and trailer up to the big field." "Don't let him drive too hard Sean," said his Uncle Gerry.Patsy of course was well under the legal age for driving a tractor. However, it was the morning time and there wouldn't be any police about so Gerry didn't object; he knew his son was very keen on driving the tractor any chance he could get and apart from his occasional tendency to drive a little quicker than he ought to, he could manoeuvre the tractor and trailer around the narrow roads pretty well.

At the turn of the key, the engine roared into life and the two cousins, Patsy in the driving seat and Sean at his side, made their way to the 'big field". There was a bit of a bump at the entry to the field, but Patsy negotiated the entry slowly in a low gear and they got the trailer through the narrow gate-entry with inches to spare. It would be a good forty-five minutes before the baler would arrive. Patsy turned off the engine. The hay had been turned the previous morning and had a good days drying yesterday. They had been lucky this year weatherwise – the year before had been rainy in patches. Patsy drove the tractor down to the bottom of the field and parked on a piece of hard, stony ground. He switched off the engine. About fifteen minutes later a cyclist dismounted at the field entrance, set his bicycle beside the gate and made his way towards the two cousins. "Hi Kevin, good to see you're early boy," shouted Patsy. "I hadn't much option – there was some boy operatin' a pneumatic drill about twenty yards from our house this mornin'. Where's everybody else?" "The baler won't be comin' until eleven." "I take it there'll be a bit of help comin' as well. I mean – I don't mind givin' ye's a hand but a ten-hour shift wasn't exactly what I had in mind." "It 'll be good for ye Kev.,",said Patsy. "Ye'll be all fit and tanned 'n the women 'll be chasin' ye up the street." "They'll be callin' you the fit farmer," laughed Sean."This 'll be as near as I ever get to bein' a farmer," said Kevin. "Up every mornin', Sundays included, rain, sleet or snow, milkin, cows, diggin' spuds, liftin' hay. All that hard work would put ye in an early grave." "I'd far rather have it than bein' stuck all day on a buildin' site, or even worse – in a bloody office, havin' some prat tellin' ye what to do all the time," replied Patsy. " There's no such thing as a perfect job," opined Sean "Oh aye there is",said Kevin. "Playin' for Celtic or even Liverpool. Playin' football and gettin' paid for it and the best thing is - ye've the whole summer off to do what ye want." "Well – if ye ever make the big-time Kevin, ye're always welcome back in our hayfield for a bit of summer relaxation," joked Patsy. "Are ye seriously thinkin' of playin' soccer for a livin' once ye leave school?" asked Sean. "Ye'll have to travel over the water and there's not that many that actually make it you know Kevin." "Ye never know if ye don't try," said Kevin."I'm goin, to give it a go." "You'll end up marryin' some English doll and your weins 'll grow up talkin' in Cockney accents just like them Brits that stopped us yesterday," retorted Patsy. "As long as she's got blond hair and big tits, I don't care if her and the weins are all dumb," replied Kevin and Sean and Patsy laughed. "What about youse two – are ye not thinkin' of gettin' out of this country when ye get a bit older?" asked Kevin. "I'd be happy enough helpin' the oul' fella on the farm and playin' Gaelic, maybe for the county," said Patsy. "If ye keep at it Patsy – ye'll be playin' for the county be-fore you're twenty," replied Kevin. Football, Gaelic or soc-cer, was one topic which Kevin took absolutely seriously. "What about you, oul' brainbox," asked Patsy of his cous-in, referring to the fact that Sean had got the second highest mark in maths in the summer class tests. "I haven't a bloody clue," retorted Sean. "You could be an accountant or' somethin', Sean" said Kevin, "and show me and Patsy how to fiddle our taxes."

The three boys chatted on for a while. About 11 o'clock, the tractor with the baler behind it entered the field. The driver, a local farmer called Barney Maguire, steered the tractor down to the bottom, near to where the boys were sitting. He waved to them and proceeded to the far corner. He slowly made his way up the edge of the field and the first bale appeared from the tail of the baler. The boys, who were in no big hurry to start, let him go the whole way up before slowly ambling towards where the first bale had dropped. "There's the reinforcements arrivin' now," observed Sean. His father had parked their blue Volkswagen Beetle over on the grass verge on the other side of the road and Peter and Gerry were making their way down. "Hi Sean – are none of your sisters comin' to give us a hand?" asked Kevin. "They were goin' to come only they heard you were a wee pervert and changed their minds," replied Sean as he tossed Kevin's hair with his hands. Patsy giggled as he lifted the bale out from the edge of the field – "Ahh, I hate those big heavy bastards at the side – they rip the s--t out of yer fingers!" Owing to the fact that the grass at the side of the field didn't get as much sun because of the hedge, the bales tended to be heavier, and Sean usually dragged them by the side rather than lifting them by the rope.

"Hi – did I tell ye's about the face I got on the last night of the youth club,"said Kevin in a quiet, entrez-nous tone, as he didn't want his friends' fathers overhearing the conversation. The youth-club in Lamagh which Sean and Patsy both went to occasionally, had closed for the summer, but both of them had missed the last night. "Naw – who was it?" replied an intrigued Patsy. Before Kevin could reply, Peter and Gerry came over to join them. Sean and Patsy would have to wait for a while before they would hear Kevin's tale of romance. "Hello Kevin – thank for comin' out to keep an eye on these boys," joked Peter. "How are ye doin' Mr Daly. Good day for the job," replied Kevin. "Aye – hope it keeps that way. How's yer mother keepin' these days." "She's not doin' too bad," replied Kevin. Kevin's father had passed away the year before of a heart-attack and Kevin's mother had found it hard to cope. His father had only been fifty-four years of age and Kevin was the youngest of five children. Although his father had a bit of a gambling problem, Kevin had been hit hard by his father's premature demise.

The five workers now started their days work in earnest. The bales would have to be built into little stacks of seven – two on the bottom, cut side down;two on top of them at 90degrees; two on top of that the same way as the first two and finally, one on top. The main job of the three boys was to bring the bales nearer each other so the two men could do the building. Sean was glad that it was a little cooler than yesterday. They proceeded slowly and methodically up the field. The conversation had died down for the time being as everyone concentrated on the job to be done.

Shortly before two o'clock, a few more people arrived at the field. Sean recognised them from a distance. It was his Uncle Philip, who was married to Aunt Teresa, his father's younger sister. With him was his nine-year old son Thomas; a talkative, inquisitive child, if ever there was one. Thomas was too young to do any work - he just hung around the older boys and chatted incessantly, not caring whether he was being listened to or not. If none of the boys would answer one of his questions, he would ask another one. The previous year Patsy had found a frog and threw it at him. That had shifted him temporarily, but he still came back. Philip, who was short and a little overweight, greeted his wife's brothers. He owned a grocers shop in Lisgannon and normally worked on Saturdays but had taken the day off at Teresa's insistence. He was a jovial, friendly man and Sean quite liked him. He was quite different to his aunt Teresa, who was small, red-haired and quite sharp with her tongue. "What job would ye have for me?" asked Philip. "Peter has to go into Lamagh," said Gerry, "so you can help us put a load on the trailer and we'll take it down to the shed." "Can I stay here Daddy?" pleaded Thomas. "Aye ye can son – but stay away from the baler." "You'se keep an eye on him – we'll be back in an hour," instructed Peter. The three men went off to load the trailer. The three boys continued building, as most of the bales wouldn't be lifted until at least the next day and they couldn't be sure that the weather wouldn't break. "Patsy – if you throw any frogs at me – I'll tell my daddy on you." "I don't think there's any frogs in this field Thomas – would ye like a spider instead?"

"DADDY- DADDY," squealed Thomas. "He's only car-
ryin' on," reassured Sean. "He dosen't have any spiders."
With the three men away, Patsy now had the chance to
ask Kevin the question he had asked him earlier. He was
especially curious as he suspected he knew the answer.
"Who did ye face at the youth club Kevin?" asked Patsy
quietly, trying to keep out of Thomas's earshot. "I'll give
ye a guess." "Geraldine Donnelly." "Naw – even better
lookin'." "It wasn't Collette McCann was it." A big smile
came over Kevins face. "You lucky bastard – I got her under the mistletoe at Christmas but her oul' fella's always
waitin' outside for her in the car at 11 o'clock." Not on the
last night he wasn't – she was stayin' over with the Dev-
lins that night." "They live over the street from you, don't
they?" "I think ye're getting' the picture now," replied a
smiling Kevin. "What was it you were sayin' last night
about about livin' out here in the country Patsy," laughed
Sean. "Where did ye take her to – did ye get much?" inquired Patsy who had forgotten about bales for the time
being. "I couldn't take her inside - me ma was up. I just
faced her up against the wall at the back of the house." "
I bet she didn't let ye get anythin'". " I got her bra off – it
took a bit o'coaxin' and some awkward fingerwork, but
I managed it". "Did ye get any more than that". "I was
workin' on that but the Devlin sisters came out lookin'
for her," replied Kevin. Sean knew that Patsy fancied Collette McCann himself. He fancied her a bit too though he
fancied Geraldine Donnelly more. Interested as he was in
Kevin's story, he couldn't help noticing that young Tho-

mas, who rarely shut up, was standing a few yards away from them and actually keeping quiet. "Thomas – why don't you go and hide and I'll try and find ye," suggested Sean. "Naw – I don't like playing hide-and-seek." Patsy and Kevin continued to share stories about girls. Sean was glad that neither of them had managed to get off with Geraldine Donnelly, but he was uncomfortable about the fact that Thomas was overhearing the conversation. "Thomas – could you go down 'n get the bottle of water sittin' on the back of the trailer," requested Sean. "Naw – couldn't be bothered." "Jaysus – look what I see," exclaimed Patsy. "What?" "A great big slimy – FROG!" shouted Patsy. Thomas had a look of terror on his face as he took to his heels. "That shifted the wee bugger," laughed Patsy. "I don't think ye should have done that Patsy," said Sean. The conversation drifted onto other matters and Thomas went on his merry way walking around the field. Sean warned him to keep well away from the baler. "There was a wee boy from near here was dragged into one last year and it made mincemeat out of him," lied Sean to his young cousin. The men returned. This time Sean's mother and his Aunt Teresa were with them. Both of the women carried baskets. It was time for a break.

Brigid poured each of the workers a cup of tea from the flask. Barney Maguire came down to join them. "Do ye take sugar Barney?" "Aye – two please Brigid." Teresa went around, offering the sandwiches which she had made earlier. "The balers goin' all right today," said Gerry to Barney. "Aye – thank God", said Barney. "There's nothin' worse than gettin' a good days weather and the bloody thing breaks down." "Another hour and ye should have it baled Barney,"said Peter. "Aye – I've a wee field o' me own to do after that," replied Barney. "Have ye got anyone to give ye a hand?" inquired Teresa. "Me brother finishes work at five so he'll be about," replied Barney. Teresa gave her young son a cuddle. "Have you been helpin' all the big boys with the hay, wee pet?" "Aye I have mammy. Mammy – guess what Patsy and Kevin were talkin' about." "I don't know son – what were they talkin' about?"

"Pullin' bras aff gerls,mammy!"

There was a momentary uneasy silence. Sean was thankful that his young cousin had omitted him and he was trying hard to suppress a burst of laughter. Never had he wanted to laugh so much. Patsy's face had gone a little pink, as had Kevin's. Teresa bristled. "You pair should be ashamed of yerselves, goin'over chat like that in front of a wein!" "Better get back to work," muttered Patsy, who was not known for getting up early from teabreaks. Kevin hastily followed him.

CHAPTER 3

Early September 1972

The summer of 1972 slowly passed by. For Sean, Patsy and Kevin, early September beckoned a return to school.

Sean was now going into his third year at the Christian Brothers College in

Lamagh. He was in the "B" class. This would be the last year in which he would study a pre-set curriculum. At the end of the year, there would be examinations, after which he would decide what subjects to study for O-Level. Apart from the obvious subjects such as English, Mathematics, Geography and History, the curriculum also included a mixture of science and languages such as Physics Chemistry, French, Irish and Latin. This year there was also one period per week of a new subject called Elocution. Sean was curious as to what this new subject might be about. Some of his classmates found Irish a bit of a handful, but Sean's weakness was most definitely the dreaded Latin. Patsy was equally incompetent at Latin, perhaps more-so, but he had a different attitude to his schoolwork than Sean, in that he didn't take it too seriously. Mastering the declensions and remembering the multitude of words beginning with "q" was always a bit of a struggle for Sean. Sometimes he wondered how two Romans meeting in a street could ever have had a chat with each other. To compound the problem, the Brother who taught the subject, Br. Francis, was a rather sarcastic character. Rather than physically punish his charges, he would subject them to his own unique brand of putdown humour and no one was spared.

On the first day back (a Friday), the boys shared stories about the events of the previous eight weeks. Some of them had been to the Gaeltacht in Donegal to further their ability to speak Irish and had had a great time. Sean told the story about Kevin and Patsy's conversation in the hayfield which a lot of his classmates found very amusing. Kevin was in no way upset about Sean's verbal recollection of this event as it portrayed him as a bit of a ladies man and indeed he was quite proud of his 'conquest'.

The timetable for the year was given out and it was much as expected. Classes were divided into thirty-five minute periods. They had four periods of P.E. in the week - two on Tuesday morning and two on Thursday evening. Sean also noted that there was a double period of Latin on Tuesday afternoon. This made him a little uneasy as it was always harder to escape the personal scrutiny of a teacher during a double period.

The boys were let out at half-day after morning Mass in the local church. Sean and his mammy went shopping on Saturday for a few books, a new pair of trousers and a new pair of shoes.

On Monday 4th September the lessons began. The first day of classes passed satisfactorily The school dinner of sausages, beans and chips which they served at the canteen every now and again was as tasty as ever. The same couldn't be said of every school dinner though. Tuesday morning was O.K. too – especially the P.E. class. The boys were divided into teams for five-a-side soccer in the gym and by the end of the period they were lathered in sweat and ready for the shower. After lunch they went to Room 3 for a double period of Sean's least favourite subject.

Br. Francis was about 5'8" tall. His main distinguishing features were his thick black hair, black glasses and an omnipresent black stubble. Sean thought he could have passed for a Roman himself as he looked not unlike some of the Italian soccer players he had seen on TV. He marched purposefully into the room holding his books under his arm. The boys were already seated. "Good morning one and all – glad to see you all again. No doubt you've all been spending a little time over the holidays casting your eye over the vocabulary section at the back of the book. It's remarkable how quickly the memory fades you know. Before we attempt a translation – and there will be quite a few of those on the syllabus for this year – let us turn to page 175 and spend a few minutes re-acquainting ourselves with some of the nouns and verbs which comprise part of the beautiful, elegant language that is Latin." Everyone turned to page 175. After ten minutes, Br. Francis told the class to shut their books. He started at the top left hand corner of the class and proceeded to question each boy in turn. "Donnelly – my red-haired friend – give me the Latin word for angry." "Iratus, sir." "From which is derived the English word irate.O.K - McCanny – what is the Latin word for the moon?" "Lunus, sir." Sean, who sat behind Noel McCanny was next. Patsy was behind him."No it is Luna – moving on to the concrete corner – Daly.S. – what is the Latin for the verb 'I listen to'." "Audio, sir". "Correct - and now moving on to Daly.P. – what is the Latin word for 'money'". As Patsy was trying to come up with an answer, Sean was relieved that he had got his right. He had been lucky as he hadn't known the answer to the first two questions. He knew the answer to Patsy's question but of course couldn't tell him. "Argent, sir." "I can see the old concrete is as solid as ever. You wouldn't be getting your languages mixed up –would you boy?" There was a ripple of laughter across the classroom. It was no more than a ripple as anyone laughing too loud would have been inviting trouble. "Daly P. – perhaps you could let your cement-brained cousin know what the Latin word for money is!""Pecunia, sir." "Correct." Thus Br. Francis made his way around the class of boys. Occasionally he would go up to the board to make a point. During the second period the boys studied about the gladiators and the chariot races. Sean much preferred this part of the syllabus to struggling with incomprehensible pieces of Latin prose.

The following morning, the first class after break-time was Elocution. Sean had asked his mother the night before if she knew what it was and she had told him that it was the art of learning how to speak correctly."Ye mean like learnin' how to talk without usin' slang – that sorta thing?", Sean inquired of his mother. "That would be part of it Sean – but ye also have to learn to pronounce words correctly and not talk with an accent." "Do I talk with an accent?" "A wee bit son", his mother chuckled. "I don't know anybody who lives round here who dosen't." "Sounds like the teacher 'll have a busy job then",said Sean. Kevin, who was friendly with a neighbour of his from the estate who was in the 'A' class, had found out from him that the Elocution teacher was an older lady named Mrs White. Mrs White wasn't part of the school staff – she went around different schools in the area teaching school-children the art of speaking properly.

As Mrs White made her way down the corridor, Kevin whispered to Patsy in a low voice. "Let's play a trick on this oul' doll. I'll hide in the store room and you put my shoes over at the bottom of that big curtain. When she calls out my name you tell her I'm hidin' in behind the curtain." Pat-sy sniggered, quickly took Kevin's shoes from him and put them at the foot of the large curtain. Meanwhile the shoe-less Kevin proceeded to hide himself in the store-room just as Mrs White entered the room. The two boys had been sitting in the back row and nobody in the class including Sean had noticed that Kevin had gone missing.

Mrs White introduced herself to the boys. "Good morn-ing everyone. My name is Mrs White and for the next two terms I shall be having you one period a week for elocution. Because I'm not familiar with your names, I shall use the roll-book for the next few weeks when asking questions. Now – does anyone now what elocution is – and that is a question for Mr McGonigle." Brian McGonigle – a stout, ruddy-faced publicans son replied "Learnin' how to talk right Miss." "Yes – or to put it more eloquently – elocution is the art of clear and expressive speech. A person who has been trained in elocution will speak English without using slang. Neither should they speak with any detectable accent or in a particular dialect. What do we mean by slang -ah Mr McCanny." "Not talkin' English the right way Miss." "Yes – or to put it another way – using words which are informal - for example – does anyone now what the correct term for a bookie is – Mr McKenna." "Bookmaker miss." "That's right - bookie is the slang word. Now – does anybody know what the difference between accent and dialect is. Mr Convery – do you know the difference between accent and dialect?" "Well – I know that accent means the sound of the way that ye talk Miss." "Well – that's one out of two. What about dialect – does anyone know what that term means?" Nobody put up their hand "A dialect is a variety of English that is distinct from other varieties. Although dialects are usually recognisable from the speaker's accent, the term mainly implies differences of grammar. Now – could someone give me an example of a phrase which could be said to be dialectual – Mr O'Neill?" There was no reply.

"Ah – Mr O'Neill must be absent today. Let's s". "I think he might be behind that curtain Miss," exclaimed Patsy. Mrs White looked to her right and noticed a pair of shoes protruding from the bottom of the curtain. "Mr O'Neill - perhaps you could stop playing childish games and come out from behind that curtain and take your seat in the class!" Patsy – who by now had his hand over his mouth was trying hard to suppress laughter. Thankfully Mrs White was totally focused on the curtain rather than him. The rest of the boys in the class thought that Kevin was behind the curtain. There were a few giggles and some of the boys on the far side of the classroom were in a semi-standing position trying to see Kevin's shoes. Mrs White, who until now had been a model of stoic professionalism, was becoming less stoical by the minute. "Young man – you may think you are being funny, but I can assure you that you are not. Now – if you don't come out from behind that curtain within the next ten seconds – I shall be reporting you to the vice-principal. I'm going to start counting now. Ten, nine, eight, seven, six, five, four." There was a slight pause by Mrs White. "Three" was uttered much more slowly and deliberately. "Two" was given the same significance. "One". Everybody except Patsy wondered whether Kevin was about to appear from behind the curtain. "Right young man – this game is over!" shouted Mrs White angrily as she proceeded to make her way to the vice-principal's office.

"Miss – maybe he's not in behind that curtain atall," suggested Brian McGonigle. Mrs White, perhaps realising that she could make a fool of herself in front of the vice-principal, made an abrupt change of direction and proceeded to pull back the curtain with some gusto. Kevin, who had a view of the curtain from the keyhole of the store-room, could barely contain himself with laughter. "Does anyone know where this boy is?" shouted a red-faced Mrs White amid a cackle of riotous laughter. "Was he here before break-time" "Aye – he was miss", some-one said. "Does anyone know where he is now?" Patsy of course knew, but he didn't want to tell on Kevin. He was content to let her find out for herself, if she could.

Realising that these were probably Kevin's shoes and that he therefore couldn't be too far away, Mrs White decided to have a look for him in the store-room. Kevin, of course, saw her coming through the keyhole. She opened the door - nothing there. She was about to close the door again when she realised that she perhaps ought to check behind the door. "Get back into that classroom young man!" shouted a red-faced Mrs White to a shoeless Kevin. There was more laughter as a sheepish-faced Kevin retrieved his shoes and went to his seat. "You can be sure that for the remainder of this year – I will not be tolerating any nonsense from practical jokers. Mr O'Neill – please report to the vice-principals office after lunch-break."

Mrs White regained her composure and the rest of the class was conducted without incident.

CHAPTER 4

Early October 1972.

In the month of October, farmers in.Northern.Ireland were mainly pre-occupied with one activity – potato-gathering. Sean had mixed feelings about potato-gathering. On one hand – it was a chance to earn a bit of money. On the other - the work was so tedious and backbreaking that it was nearly tempting to try and make an excuse to avoid it. You couldn't hide from the work in a potato-field. Also there was an element of competition among the potato-gatherers to see who could gather the most bags and you definitely didn't want to end up with less bags than your pals. Sean and Patsy gathered for Gerry and he paid them 15p a bag - the same as all the rest of the young lads. Gerry wasn't a big-time potato farmer but, other than Patsy, he had only one man to help him and that meant that there was no shortage of work to be done. The only time you could get away from the field before 6 o'clock was whenever it rained. A couple of hours after school during the week wasn't too bad, but Saturday was an eight-hour day with only two tea-breaks and Sean found the last couple of hours on a Saturday always went very slowly. This year he had a special reason for wanting to earn a bit of money. He had seen an electric guitar in a music shop in the town on the day that his mother had taken him shopping for the school-uniform. The colour and shape of it had intrigued him and some nights, as he lay listening to music on Radio Luxembourg on his small transistor radio, he dreamed of owning it. The pop music he liked best was by bands which had a guitar player – bands like Sweet and Slade. He also noticed that girls his age seemed to have romantic notions about pop-stars they had never met nor seen. Geraldine Donnelly had told him once that she had a big poster of David Cassidy in her bedroom. Sean - unlike Patsy or Kevin, was a bit shy with girls and he secretly hoped that if the girls thought he was a guitar-player they would make the first move. As far as his chances with Geraldine Donnelly were concerned – well there was some hope, as David Cassidy would hardly ever be moving to Co. Tyrone. His plan was to save up enough money to buy a secondhand electric guitar and then ask his mammy to buy an amplifier for him for his birthday. He knew next to nothing about guitars or amplifiers so he intended to get a couple of magazines over the next couple of weeks and suss out what would be best to buy. He'd have to ask his mammy pretty soon or she'd end up buying him a coat or a pair of shoes. His birthday wasn't until the 24th October when he'd be 14. So one evening in early October, knowing that his parents weren't terribly enamoured with the musical idiom that was 'glitter rock', he put the question delicately to his mother.

"Ah ma – I've been meanin' to ask ye – ye know me birthday's comin' up soon and ah – I've been thinkin' of getting' somethin' different this year for meself but ah-". "What have ye been thinkin' of buying son?" his mother interjected. "Well – ye mind that day we were shoppin' in Lamagh - I happened to notice a guitar in a shop winda and – well I've been thinkin' of buyin' one with the money

I earn from the spuds." "Well – I don't have any objection to that son – it would be nice to have a musician in the family – your granny was musical ye know." "But this isn't just an ordinary guitar ma – it's an electric one." "What! – ye mean like those long-haired galloots who look like women play on the TV! I thought ye meant the ordinary guitar that ye strum that that fella Don McLean uses. And they're so loud. Ye'd drive yer oul' granda and yer da spare with the noise!"

"But I can practise out in the shed ma – the thing is ma – I only can gather up enough money to buy the guitar – I was hopin' you could buy me the amplifier as a birthday present." "I'll have to ask yer father, Sean. God – and I thought ye were a sensible wee fella. You'll not be growin' yer hair down yer back and puttin' on lipstick I hope." "Ye wouldn't get away with that livin' around here ma – well definitely not the lipstick anyway," quipped Sean. "Well – yer father should be home in about half-an hour and I'll have a wee chat with him about it. Now – don't forget about yer homework." "God bless ye ma," said Sean and gave his mother a hug.

When Peter came home, Brigid always gave him time to clean, eat and unwind before bringing up anything she wanted to discuss with him. "Peter," she said, "Sean and I were havin' a wee chat this evening, about what he wanted for his birthday." "Well – did he mention anything in particular," responded Peter. "He did actually – somethin' a bit unusual." "What like?" "Well – when I took him shoppin' for his school stuff a few weeks ago - he saw this electric guitar in a shop winda. He wants to buy it with the money he'll get from the potatoes and he wants us to buy an amplifier for him." "Well – pickin' spuds is hard work and if he wants that guitar bad enough we'll buy him the amplifier." Brigid was surprised at how easily Peter had agreed to buy the amplifier. " Well – that's settled then – to tell ye the truth – I didn't think you'd be terribly happy about it." "Well – he'll have to practise out in the shed and I'll not be comin' out to listen to him. But in a way I'm glad." "Why's that?",inquired Brigid. "Because he hasn't got any hobbies. He's not into football the same way Patsy is. The thing that would worry me in a couple of years time is that he could end up gettin' involved with the IRA. We'll just have to warn him as best we can, but if he has a hobby he feels passionately about, there's a lesser chance of that happenin'." "Jesus – you scare me when you say that Peter." "Well – I don't mean to love – but ye have to be realistic about what's happenin' in this country at the minute. After what happened at the start of the year on Bloody Sunday – the Civil-Rights Movement is dead and buried. The Stormont Government might be dead and buried too - but Catholics aren't gettin' an even slice of the pie and there won't be any peace in this country until they do." "Kathleen told me that one time that she saw a 'No Catholic Need Apply' sign on a shop winda." "And for every employer who puts up a sign like that – there's probably ten more who feel the same way -though they may not advertise it in public." "Well then – it looks like we're goin' to have a musician of a sort in the family then," said Brigid.

"I must say - I would have preferred him to want to get an ordinary guitar and learn to sing a few songs." "Could yer blessin's Brigid – it could have been a drum kit he'd have been lookin' for." "Aww God! - heaven forbid. Don't let him hear ye say that in case he changes his mind."

The following day Brigid let Sean know the good news. "Thanks very much ma," said Sean. "Don't worry about the noise – I'll not turn up too loud." "And don't be cuttin' short yer homework to practise either Sean.Yer education comes first ye know." "I know ma. When can we go back into Lamagh then?" "We'll go sometime in November. I know yer birthday's before that but the spuds won't be fin-ished before the end of October." Sean celebrated the good news by playing a little bit of air-guitar, thus receiving a quizzical look from his mother. "By the way – are ye goin' to teach yerself or do ye intend to take lessons?" "Well - I intend to get a tutor book. The music teacher at school plays guitar in a folk-group so maybe I could talk him into showin' me a few chords and stuff. There's no guitar-les-sons in music class or anythin' like that." "Well – if ye're interested - ye'll learn. Now – could ye take yer granda up that tea and toast I made for him. " Sean did as his mother asked and went to bed a very happy young man.

Chapter 5

Saturday 14th October 1972

It was a cold, clear mid-autumn morning. Between working after school and full day on the previous two Saturdays, Sean was almost forty pounds richer than he had been at the start of the month. He had the money stacked away in a small biscuit tin in his bedroom and some nights before he went to bed he would count it. It wasn't that he thought any of his sisters would steal it on him; it just made him feel good to think that, as every week of autumn passed, he was one step nearer to achieving his goal. It was cloudy and windy today, but at least it was dry and he didn't want to see any rain before 4 o'clock if possible. His muscles had been broken in by the toil and exertion of the previous fortnight and he didn't feel nearly as stiff now as he had at the beginning of October. He had learned from the year before that it was better to break yourself in with a couple of days gathering after school before doing a full day on a Saturday. There were eight other gatherers in the field today, including his two sisters Siobhan and Mary with two of their classmates from the convent. Neither of them was particularly good-looking, thought Sean. One of them was a large, fattish girl called Grainne who had red hair and a larger than average posterior, the size of which became particularly apparent when she assumed potato-gathering position. The other one was a pale, thin girl called Bronagh. Patsy and Kevin were both gathering further down the field behind him. Noel McCanny and Brian McGonigle were gathering he drill on the opposite side. His Uncle Gerry was digging the drills and a local man, Hughie Scullion, who helped Gerry occasionally, was keeping an eye on the digger to stop it getting clogged with weeds. Hughie also helped Gerry load the filled bags onto the trailer.

It was work like this that convinced Sean that, whatever the future held for him, farming was out of the question. Indeed, he shared the opinion which Kevin had stated in the hayfield back in the summertime, that there was just too much hard, backbreaking work involved. As repetitive an activity as potato-gathering was, you couldn't allow yourself to daydream for any extended period of time or the next thing you would know, Patsy and Kevin would be two bags ahead of you. Also, the drills could only be dug as quickly as the slowest gatherer would allow and nobody wanted to be seen as a slowcoach, especially when there were girls gathering.

About one-o'clock it was time for the first tea-break. Kathleen had arrived with the flasks and the gatherers made their way towards the top end of the field. As there were no facilities for washing muddy hands, Sean was careful not to let any specks of mud into his filled teacup. He also held the sandwich by the crust for the same reason. "Anybody that wants sugar – just help yourselves to it," instructed his aunt. "How many bags are ye up now Brian?" asked Kevin to his classmate. "Thirteen," said Brian. "What about yerself?" "I'm on me fourteenth at the minute – what about you Sean?" "I've just finished me fourteenth. What about you Noel?" Noel – who was only on his second day out gathering,replied, "I'm on me fourteenth too," knowing that he was only in fact on his twelfth bag. "What about ye's girls – how are ye gettin' on with the spuds today?" inquired Kevin. "None of your business ye wee skiter," replied big Grainne. "Jesus – did somebody bite the head off yer teddy-bear?" replied Kevin. "Ye only want to know how many bags we've gathered be-cause ye think ye've gathered more than we have, but we're not racing against one another the way you lot are,"said Bronagh. "I'm not racin' agin' anybody,"lied Kevin. There was a short lull in the conversation as the hungry workers ate their sandwiches and drank their tea.

"Did ye see Marc Bolan on Top of the Pops on Thurs-day night Grainne?"asked Mary. "Aye – I saw him. I like his song but he's not as good-lookin' as Donny Osmond. I think he's lovely." Suddenly Kevin broke into song. "And they calllled it Puppeee Laaavvve." Kevin's classmates started laughing. "God – imagine there are people who go out and buy crap like that,"remarked Kevin. "You're the one who's full of crap," replied Grainne. "Donny Os-mond's a pansy," said Kevin. "He's not a pansy – he does karate and he could beat the shite out of you." "I'd be more afeard of them big white teeth of his. He could take a quare bite out of ye!" "At least he's got white teeth – not a deeper shade of yella – like yer own," retorted Grainne. Clearly big Grainne could hold her own in a slanging match, thought Sean. Kevin must have thought so too as he changed the subject, perhaps regretting that he had for-gotten to brush his teeth that morning. "Is anybody goin' to the Hallowee'n disco?" asked Kevin. "I'll be goin' – if me oul' boy lets me," said Brian. "Don't forget to ask him for a carryout of beer for yerself and yer mates," joked Patsy. "It's a fancy-dress do isn't it?" "Aye it is - same as last year." "What will you be goin' as Siobhan ?" asked Kevin. "I dunno Kevin – maybe I'll go as Donny Osmond's sister," laughed Siobhan. "Hi Brian – you could go as wee Jimmy Osmond," laughed Kevin. Everyone seemed to find this funny except Brian who didn't care for being thought of as a Jimmy Osmond lookalike. "Aye – well you could go as that boy that plays the guitar in Slade with the big buck teeth and the lipstick." "I know what I'm goin' as," said Kevin, "but I'm not tellin' anybody." Sean, who had been thinking about little else other than his electric guitar since the start of October, had pretty much forgot about the disco. Now he was going to have to give his fancy-dress a bit of thought in the coming week.

"Right – are we ready to start again soon?" said Gerry. As the workers slowly got to their feet, Kevin whispered to Sean and Patsy, "Wait till the big doll starts to gather again and see if we can hit her on the ars with a spud." "Who's goin' to shoot first?" asked Sean. "I will - and if I miss, some o' youse throw one after me." As big Grainne bent down to gather the potatoes she had left in her section of the drill before teabreak was called, Kevin lifted a small potato and threw it. Though Grainne's bottom presented an adequate target, Kevin's shot, perhaps made more with power than accuracy in mind, landed several feet from her. It didn't stop her from looking around her shoulder though. Kevin whispered to Sean, "Right - you try." Sean, who suspected that big Grainne would be intent on retribution, decided that he would make sure that Grainne wouldn't see him. He lifted another small white potato, took careful aim and immediately the potato had left his hand, assumed potato-gathering position. He didn't even see the potato hit Grainne square on target. The other two did however and chuckled to themselves. As big Grainne assumed upright position, she looked around and noticed Patsy and Kevin giggling. She threw down her basket and made her way towards the two boys. Sean could see out of the corner of his eye that she was clearly quite angry. "Ye wee bastard - wait till I catch ye!" shouted a clearly upset Grainne. Her pace quickened as she got nearer Kevin and it became clear to Kevin and the others that she was blaming him. "Some of ye's hold him for me!" shouted Grainne. Brian McGonigle, who was giggling himself, caught Kevin in a bear-hug from behind. "McGonigle – let me go ye big bastard," pleaded Kevin who was caught firmly in the bigger boy's strong grip. "It wasn't me – it was him," panted Kevin as he nodded his head in Sean's direction. Because his arms were pinned to his sides, he couldn't point Sean out. It wouldn't have mattered anyway as Grainne had already pronounced him guilty. Brian let him go just as Grainne caught his arm and wrestled him to the ground. "It wasn't me!" repeated Kevin who clearly wasn't enjoying this large girl sitting on top of him. "It was you – I saw ye throw the first one," replied Grainne. "I'm goin' to give ye a wee massage – would ye like that?" she inquired as she lifted a piece of soft sticky clay. "Naww –don't - ahhh Jaysuss!" exclaimed Kevin as big Grainne rubbed the clay around his neck and down the front of his tee-shirt. She then rubbed what was left of the clay on his face. "That'll teach ye – ye boy ye!" remarked Grainne, who, satisfied with her revenge, got to her feet and walked back to her drill. Once she was out of earshot, a dirty-faced Kevin picked himself up. "That big doll could rassle Mick Mc-Manus," he muttered. "She's the junior shot-putt champion at the convent," replied Sean. "Maybe I should have told ye that before ye got yer bright idea." "Maybe we should stop talkin' about her or she might come back,"joked Patsy. "I think she had it in for me after I insulted Donny Osmond," noted Kevin.

"Have you boys not got some work to do?" shouted Gerry from the cab of the tractor. The three took their pre-teabreak positions and work resumed as normal.

Chapter 6

Thursday 26th October

For Sean and all his schoolmates, the main event of Halloween was the fancy-dress disco. For the boys in the town, another source of entertainment was door-rapping, though out in the country where the houses were farther apart and nearly every house had a long lane or a cross dog (or both), it wasn't done as much. Also, the parents of the area would have strongly disapproved of their children tormenting their neighbours – especially elderly people who lived alone. Sean remembered too that in the late 1960's, before the Troubles started, fireworks could be bought in the local shops. He remembered his father bringing home a selection of squibs, rockets and Catherine wheels to light in the back garden and he recalled the distinctive, pungent smell that lingered after the firework had been lit.

Back to the present though, and solving a problem more often encountered by members of the female gender – what to wear? If only he had a guitar he could borrow his sister Mary's wig and dress himself as Marc Bolan, the pop-star. Still – the guitar would be damaged as there would be no safe place for it with everyone jumping about and dancing. Suddenly an idea grabbed him. Why not make a dummy guitar with some wood, paint and a black marker to colour in the strings? His daddy had a small workshop at the back of the house, with a vice and some tools. There was a strip of wood about one-and-a-half inches thick which could be used for the neck. His sister had a big poster of Bolan with his guitar in her bedroom and he could use that as a plan to shape the guitar-body. Time to get to work! Working out how to look like Bolan could come later, but his sister Mary was a big fan and she could give him some help and advice. There was only five days to go so he went out to the shed right away and laid down the basic design for the dummy guitar. Drawing the strings onto the neck would be fairly easy. The awkward bits would be joining the neck to the body and making a headstock to join to the neck. He'd have to get his da to help him. Peter, who had spotted the light in the shed and had gone in to turn it off, appeared behind him. "Da – will ye help me make somethin'?" "What are ye lookin' to make, son?" "I want to put together a dummy guitar for this fancy-dress disco on Tuesday night." "That's a bit short-notice son." "Well – it doesn't have to be anything fancy – here's what I'm thinkin' of doin'". Sean explained the layout to his father who agreed to fashion the body of the guitar. Then they worked out a way to join the neck to the body using four small screws. At 11o'clock, Peter said "I think we'll have somethin' ready by Tuesday night Sean. We'll call it a night." "Ok da – thanks for helpin' me out." "No problem – I only hope it dosen't fall apart come Tuesday."

The following evening after school, Sean was back in the workshop. He had the Bolan poster with him as he wanted to copy the headstock design from it, or get as near to it as he could. The guitar on the poster was a beautifully contoured shape with a red and yellow body. On the head-stock of the guitar he could see the words "Gibson" and "Les Paul", written in italic writing. The first two periods next morning at school were woodwork and he'd asked the teacher to borrow a piece of discarded pine with which he hoped to fashion the headstock from. When he arrived home from school on Friday afternoon, Sean went straight out to the workshop. He drew an outline of the headstock on the piece of pine with the marker, put it in the vice and proceeded to cut away the outline with a coping saw. It took nearly an hour to do. At one point his mother had called him in to do his homework but he told her that he was doing a woodwork assessment. He then wrapped a slice of rough sandpaper around a small piece of wood and proceeded to sand the rough edges of the newly fash-ioned headstock. Though he preferred the practical side of woodwork to the theoretical side, he'd never really been passionate about the subject until now. He then took a 6" ruler and marked the points of the 6 machine heads with a pencil which he drew in with a black marker. He then cut a groove in the headstock and joined the neck to the end of the groove by applying some wood-glue. He tightened the finished article in a vice and left it overnight to harden.

On Sunday evening, Sean knocked on his sister Mary's door. "Is that you Sean?" she called. "Aye- Mary. Mary, I've been meaning to ask you a favour." "You're bound to be loaded after all potato-gathering you've been doin', Sean." "Naw – I'm not lookin' for a lend of money." "Well

– what is it then?" "Ye know this fancy-dress disco this Friday. Well I've been thinkin' of goin' as Marc Bolan. In fact I've already started makin' a dummy guitar. But I need your help to dress up like him and ye know he wears stuff on his face an all." "What put in in yer head to dress like Mark.Bolan I didn't even know ye liked him." "Well – I don't mind him. Some of his songs are OK. To tell ye the truth it was he only thing I could think of and I know you've got a curly-haired wig I could wear with one of yer white blouses." "I have. Mind you – I was thinkin' of goin' as Yvonne Goolagong the tennis player with that wig." "Could ye not go as Chris Evert instead. Goolagong is an Aborigine y'know. It'd be easier to look like Evert." "S'pose I could do that OK. Leave it to me and I'll get ye dressed up like Marc." "God bless ye, Mary," replied Sean.

The following evening when Sean came home from school he set about painting the guitar body. His father had finished shaping the body the night before for him and he had done a pretty accurate job with it. Sean decided that, instead of trying to copy the red and yellow colour of the guitar in the Bolan poster, he'd use a tin of blue paint perched up on one of the shelves. He had seen blue guitars in magazines and all rock-stars owned more than one guitar, he reasoned. He mixed some turpentine into the blue paint, stirred it well and began to apply the paint in even strokes along the wood grain, taking care to wipe any dust off the body first with a cloth. After doing the front and back, he left it to dry for a couple of hours. He then gave both sides a second coating. Rather than paint the edges, he would get a roll of black, plastic adhesive tape in town the next day and do the edges with that. He took the headstock and neck out of the vice and waved it in the air a few times to see if the headstock flew off. It stayed on OK. So, the only piece of woodwork left to do was to join the neck to the guitar-body. Peter had cut a groove at the appropriate position so Sean reckoned he could let his father do that bit for him, given that he had already started it. He would draw in the pickups, the bridge, the switches and the strings the next day when the paint had thoroughly dried and everything was joined together.

He met his father in the yard as he was coming out of the shed. "Can I show ye what I've done here, da?" "Let me see son." "Could you do that bit there, da?" "Aye – I'll do that for ye son. I'll join it with four wee screws from the back, so ye won't see them from the front. I'll do it tonight so ye can finish off everythin' yerself tomorrow evenin'"."That'd be great, da."

Lying in bed that night, Sean was thinking about all sorts of things. Mainly he was trying to think up a plan for asking Geraldine Donnelly out. He knew she'd be there and this was the perfect chance. He was also a bit worried about making a fool of himself by dressing up as an effeminate looking popstar, as he instinctively knew that he wasn't possessed of the same confident, extrovert personality as Patsy or Kevin. But then he reasoned that everyone, not just himself, would be in fancy-dress. He also had an idea to play a trick on his Granda by not saying anything to him to see if his Granda could recognise him in fancy-dress without hearing his voice.

On Tuesday afternoon, Sean bought the roll of PVC tape on the way home from school. After finishing his dinner, he went out to the workshop. His father had done just as he had promised. The "guitar" was sitting on the bench ready for completion.After admiring his father's tidy woodworking skills, he set about putting the PVC tape around the edge of the body. He had two black markers; a thin one to draw in the strings, which he did by using a spirit-level; and a thicker one to draw the bridge and switches to the body. He looked at his watch when he was finished. It was nearly eight o'clock. He really appreciated that his father had gone out of his way to take the time and trouble to help him and was eager to show him the finished article. He noticed that his father has even screwed on two small screws at opposite ends of the guitar to attach a strap to; something he himself had forgotten about.

At six o'clock on Tuesday evening, Sean and his two sisters were all focused entirely on achieving the same objective; making their fancy-dresses look as realistic as possible. Mary, who had long blonde hair like Chris Evert, didn't have to wear a wig. So, apart from getting her tennis outfit to fit, she was mainly preoccupied with getting her skin to glisten a golden–brown colour like Miss Evert's. "I'll sort you out as soon as I've got this stuff on Sean," shouted Mary from her bedroom as she applied the orange-coloured fake-tan to her left thigh. Sean was busy cleaning an old pair of his big sisters platform shoes, which he intended to wear. They were a little tight but a surprisingly good fit nonetheless. He'd have to be careful if he was up dancing, though. His other sister Siobhan was going as a nurse.

About an hour later, Mary, having checked herself in the mirror for at least the thirtieth time, emerged from the bedroom. "Ye really look the part Mary, but I hope for your sake that it dosen't rain on ye tonight. Things could get a bit messy if that orangey stuff starts to dribble onto yer tennis outfit." "Just as well ye said that Sean. I'll remember to bring me rain-mac with me. Now; let's get ye dressed up." Mary took Sean into the room and sat him down facing the mirror where she did her own make-up. His face was clean, as he had bathed an hour previously. Firstly she rubbed on some moisturiser, followed by a little foundation. She then applied some blusher to either cheek. For Sean, this was a new and somewhat un-nerving experience. Even the perfume-like smell in the room was foreign to him. This was followed by the application of a little mascara to both eyelashes, Mary expertly dabbing away any excess with a small piece of cotton wool. Finally, she applied a little lip-gloss and the make-up phase of the transformation was completed.

"Now – let's try on this wig!" said Mary. By now Siobhan had entered the room in her nurse outfit and was enthusiastically offering Mary advice. "Well – what do ye think?" she asked, pointing at the Bolan poster on the wall. "Not too far away?" "It's as near as I'll get – or want to get. Next year I'll go as a cowboy or caveman or somethin'". "Aw Sean – don't be scared to get in touch with yer feminine side," joked Siobhan, as she stroked his wig.

"Siobhan could you go out and get me the guitar. It's out in the shed. I don't want Granda seein' me 'till I'm leavin'". "Why not?" "I want to see if he'll recognise me. My voice'll give me away if I have to speak to him." "We'll call ye Fidelma," laughed Mary. "Put a tee-shirt under that blouse to keep warm Sean. It's a cold night," instructed Siobhan, as she went to fetch the guitar.

Chapter 7

Halloween Night 1972.

The disco started at 9 o'clock, so at half-past eight all three of the young Dalys were sitting in the living-room, waiting for their father to leave them into town. Granda was in his usual seat watching the TV. Finally Peter appeared. "All ready everybody?" "Ready as we'll ever be," said Mary excitedly as she made for the door to the front porch, outside where the car was sitting. "Bye Granda – come on Fidelma," said Mary to Sean. "Bye-bye love. Don't you wee hussies be stayin' out too late tonight now," replied Granda. "I'll be collectin' yous at half-eleven sharp," instructed Peter. Sean was amused by the fact that his Granda had thought he was a friend of his two sisters and did not recognise him. About two miles outside the town there was an Army checkpoint, so the journey took about twenty minutes. When they arrived, a line of people in fancy-dress were queuing outside the hall.

"Have ye's got money for the ticket?" inquired Peter. "Yes," spoke the two girls in high-pitched unison. "I'll meet ye all here at half-eleven. Have a good time." Once the three had got inside, the disco had already started. Sean's two sisters went off to look for their friends, as he did for his. His cousin Patsy had been unwell since the weekend with a dose of flu and wouldn't be here. He looked around in vain for Kevin, but with the dim lights and the fancy-dress it was hard to discern who was who. Out of the corner of his eye he saw someone come in the door. They were dressed in tight, black trousers, black tee-shirt, with a long black wig and a face decorated with co-pious amounts of mascara. The persons gait and absence of breasts indicated to Sean that it was a male. But what really made Sean laugh was the fact that around his neck he carried a large, green, rubber snake. As Sean moved closer to see who this character was, he noticed that, im-printed on the tee-shirt in Gothic writing, were the words "Schools Out For Summer". It was someone dressed as the crazy American heavy-rocker, Alice Cooper. Suddenly a flicker of recognition came over Sean's face as "Alice" stepped into the light. "Kevin – is that you?" "Hey Sean – I didn't recognise ye boy. Jesus – what have ye done with yerself?" "I could ask you the same question," laughed Sean. "Hi Sean – us big-time rock-gods are gonna pull to-night. Look – we're gettin' eyed up already." Kevin took the head of the imitation snake with its large, protruding, rubber tongue and shook it at a couple of young girls who were looking over at him. The two girls put their hands to their mouths and broke into a fit of giggling. As the song ended, the DJ said, "I see we've got Marc Bolan and Alice Cooper here tonight. Here's a couple of numbers that they might recognise." The chugging, hypnotic opening bars of "Get it On" had the immediate effect of enticing many of the female attendees up onto the dance-floor. "Hey Sean – come and dance with our two new fans." "OK. ". Sean looked around and slid his guitar under an old sofa in the corner. He wasn't just as keen as Kevin about being the centre of attention, but he went along anyway. Kevin led the way and started dancing with the taller blonde; Sean with the smaller, black-haired girl. The two were dressed as schoolgirls, with miniskirts, plaited hair and imitation freckles. "What's yer names!" shouted Kevin to the blonde, trying to make himself heard above the loud music. "I'm Juicy Lucy - she's Naughty Dotty," retorted the blonde. "Aye", laughed Kevin, "but yer real names." "I'm Fiona – she's Gemma." "Lookin' at you two makes me wish we had girls in our class," said Kevin. "Do youse two do yer own make-up?" asked Gemma, pointing to her own face to make herself understood. "I had my sister do it for me," said Sean. "Yours is a bit tidier than his. I think that friend of yours is a bit of an eejit," remarked Gemma. Midway through the song, Kevin was holding the snake in the air, pirouetting and singing the words of the chorus. Gemma looked at her bemused friend then asked Sean, "why dosen't he leave that thing down?" "He was goin' to put it under that sofa over there but he was scared it might frighten somebody," said Sean with a straight face. "I think you're as daft as he is," replied Gemma. Sean laughed. He sometimes got himself tongue-tied on the dancefloor and loud background music made chatting up girls difficult anyway. He surprised himself at his own wit. Gemma had nice eyes and Sean thought she was the prettier of the two, though Kevin probably thought otherwise.

As "Get it on" drew to a close, the DJ said, "Hey Alice – this one's for you," as the heavy power-chords of the first few bars of "School's Out For Summer" boomed out over the speakers. "Did you bring any phallic symbols with ye?" shouted Gemma to Sean. "Heh?" "Did ye bring any phallic symbols with ye?" shouted Gemma again, grinning as she spoke. Sean didn't understand the question but replied, "only a made-up guitar, lyin' under that sofa." "At least ye had the sense to leave it there." Kevin was by now in some sort of semi-trance state, oblivious to the people surrounding him. Sean hadn't realised that he was such an Alice Cooper fan. Fiona motioned to Gemma that they should go for a walk. Sean guessed that maybe she was a little miffed that Kevin wasn't paying her enough attention. " We're goin' here," motioned Gemma to Sean. "OK – I'll see ye." Just as the two girls were leaving, Sean and Kevin were joined by Noel Mc'Canny and Brian Mc'Gonigle. Mc'Gonigle was dressed as a vampire. His face was white as chalk, except for a red, imitation bloodstain around his mouth. Mc'Canny, who was an Arsenal supporter, was dressed as Charlie George, the long-haired Arsenal footballer. As Mc'Canny shook his wig-covered head and enthusiastically played air-guitar, Mc'Gonigle was waving his arms and spreading his cape whilst singing the lyrics with a strange, Bela Lugosi-like expression on his face and making clawing gestures with his hands. Gemma gave Sean an enigmatic smile as she went on her way. Did this mean that she liked him, thought Sean, or was she just giving a hint of her opinion on the sanity of "Dracula". Kevin, upon recognising his two fellow classmates, greeted them by wriggling the "snakes" head close to their faces.At the end of "Schools Out", the D.J. announced,"Well – what about one more from Alice – this is his latest one." More heavy, crunching guitar chords followed as Alice's latest hit, every bit as thunderous as the last one, belted out from the speakers.

"I'm your top prime cut of meat – I'm your choice!"

All four punched their fists in the air, singing to the chorus;

"I WANNA BE ELECTED."

"I'm your yankee doodle dandy in a gold Rolls Royce!"

"I WANNA BE ELECTED."

"Kids wanna saviour – don't need a fake!"

"I WANNA BE ELECTED."

"We're gonna rock to the rules that I make!"

"I WANNA BE ELECTED."

All four classmates were in rock'n'roll heaven and a few interested observers including a Frankenstein, a Klu-Klux-Klan Grand Wizard, and a gorilla came over to watch. All four dancers were sweating with exertion. As "Elected" drew to a close, the D.J. interjected, "Now we're going to have a change of mood folks – with a song that was No1 for five weeks in July this year. It's Donny Osmond and Puppy Love!" "I was just gettin' warmed up,"said Noel. "Me too," said Kevin. "Jesus – I'm sweatin' like a pig." "Come on and we'll sit down a minute," said Sean. "He might play some good stuff later."

The four classmates went looking for a seat. There were wooden benches at the side of the hall and a few spaces were free. As they sat down, Sean noticed that his two sisters were out dancing with two bigger fellows whom he didn't recognise. He also recognised big Grainne. She was dressed up, though it wasn't obvious to him what she was supposed to be – maybe an opera singer. "Hi Kev – there's your big woman over there." "Who!" "Big Grainne – remember the spud-gatherin'." "I didn't recognise her – I hope she dosen't recognise me either." "Ye don't fancy her then." "She might make a good dominatrix some day, but, naw – she just dosen't do it for me. That blonde I was with earlier was all right though." "Ye might be in there Kevin. Maybe ye should have paid her more attention." "Treat 'em mean – keep 'em keen Sean. Poor oul' Patsy – he'll be cheesed off about missin' this tonight." "Aye – I would have been over to see him – but I didn't want to catch the flu meself." Out of the corner of his eye Sean spied a pretty girl who immediately caught his attention. She was dressed as a Red Indian princess with her jet-black hair flowing down her back. It was Geraldine Donnelly. He experienced a sudden surge of adrenalin, coupled with butterflies in the stomach. This was a feeling he wasn't comfortable with, but he couldn't do anything about it. He deliberately said nothing to Kevin about her as he didn't want to be "slagged off" for fancying her. "Hi Sean," said Kevin excitedly as he nudged him with his elbow. No reply. "Sean – is that your Mary out on the dancefloor dressed as a tennis player?" "What?" "Is that your Mary?" "Aye." "Who's that big

fella with his arms around her?" "Dunno." "He's makin'
me a bit jealous." "She's two years older than you Kevin.
Sixteen year old girls don't go out with fourteen year old
boys. They're only interested in ye if ye're the same age
or older." "D'ye think? Jesus – she's got lovely legs, your
Mary." "She put some sort of fake-orange tan on herself
to look like Chris Evert." "She could win a prize for the
sexiest woman here the night," observed Kevin "I wonder
what time they call out the first, second and third at?"
"About half-ten I think," said Sean. "Yer man the D.J. and
the woman with him have to see everybody first." "They
give ye some money if ye win, don't they?" "Aye. D'ye
fancy yer chances?" "I dunno. I mean lookin' around ye
– anybody could win it. I suppose it's a matter of gettin'
yerself noticed," noted Kevin. "You've definitely done that
Kevin," laughed Sean. "A wee fiver would come in quare
'n' handy Sean," replied Kevin.

At about twenty-five past ten the DJ announced, "Ok - as
you all know, we're gonna give out some prizes for the best
fancy-dress costumes on display here tonight. We're gonna
call the eight finalists up onto the stage and just like the oul'
boy in Miss World – I will announce the results in reverse
order. Heh-heh." "1st one up – Frankenstein." Frankenstein
made his way up to the front, doing a stiff, awkward walk
with his arms out in front of him as everyone cheered. "2nd
one up – Alice Cooper." Kevin grabbed his snake and made
his way to the front amidst another loud cheer. "3rd one
up – Imperial Grand wizard or Mr Klu Klux Klan-Man.
Whichever ye prefer to be called mate." "4th one up – the

first female – I think anyway. It's Chris Evert." "5th one up – another lovely lady – Pocahontas." Sean's heart skipped another beat as Geraldine Donnelly walked gracefully to the stage. "6th one up - another horror-story – Dracula." "7th one up – another rock-icon – Marc Bolan." Sean – who hadn't even entertained the thought of being up on the stage, swiftly grabbed his guitar from underneath the nearby sofa and made his way to the front. "And finally – the last one up – it's Catweazle." As "Catweazle" ambled up to the front, the attendees were cheering and laughing. "Now – as I said folks – I'm gonna announce the 1st, 2nd & 3rd prizewinners in reverse order. In 3rd place – it's the King of Glam Rock – Marc Bolan." A clearly surprised Sean went forward to collect his £2 from the DJ as he crowd cheered wildly. "In 2nd place – and a prize for £3 – it's the lovely Pocahontas." A delighted Geraldine put her hands over her mouth as she stepped forward to collect her prize-money. "And now the one you've been waiting for - who is it gonna be?" he asked the audience as he cupped his hand around his ear in anticipation of an enthusiastic reply. He wasn't disappointed. There were cries of different vocal frequencies as the audience clamoured for their favorites. Catweazle, Alice and Frankenstein seemed to be among the more popular choices. "And the winner is ….," spoke the DJ as he lowered his voice, anticipating the audience's total attention. "ALICE COOPER."

For Kevin the night was going from good to better as he strutted over, imitation snake wrapped around his neck, to collect his £5. As the DJ shook hands with him, he asked

Kevin, "Well Alice - is there anything you'd like to say to the people here tonight," as he handed Kevin the microphone. "Aye – it's a dream come true y'know - an hour ago I was singin' about wantin' ta be elected – an' now I am!". "Spoken like a true politician - what do ye call the reptile?" "Gloria." "Hee-hee. Give them all a big hand folks !". The DJ led the clapping as the eight finalists made their way down the stairs.

As Sean made his way down the stairs, Geraldine was just in front of him. Sean decided that this was the chance he needed to say hello to her. "Well Geraldine – will ye be spendin' yer hard-earned money wisely?" "Sean! – aren't ye lookin' the part tonight." "So are you. I'll have to split the winnin's with our Mary though. She did me face for me." "I knew they'd vote a girl in the top three – but I thought your Mary would be the one. She really does look like Chris Evert." "She's goin' to have te soak in the bath tonight to get that stuff off her." In the background the DJ had just resumed playing records. "This is an old tearjerkin' ballad from last year – remember the Chi-Lites and 'Have you Seen her'". "Oh – I love that song," said Geraldine."D'ye fancy goin' out for a ____?" Sean was just about to finish the question when "Frankenstein" took Geraldine by the hand and said something to her like"Comin?" Geraldine waved Sean goodbye with her other hand as she was led out to the dancefloor.

Sean's heart sank. Various emotions hit him all at once. He guessed from the intimate way that they communicated that Geraldine and "Frankenstein" were boyfriend and girlfriend. He was sad, deflated, jealous and above all, sorry for himself. He walked back to the sofa, slung his guitar under it and squeezed into the last remaining space, practically wishing that the world would swallow him up. He might have been a winner at fancy-dress, but he was a loser in love, and that hurt.

As he sat in the corner of the sofa, Sean watched the couples smooch to the sound of the Chi-Lites. Kevin, who had put the snake under the sofa, was dancing with Fiona, the blonde girl he had met earlier. Mary was with the fellow she had been with earlier. He didn't see Siobhan. He found it hard to take his eyes off Geraldine and her boyfriend. They were smiling at each other, exchanging little kisses, and seemed so happy in each other's company. Sean couldn't imagine himself functioning on this level of intimacy with a girl; it was like straight out of a chapter from one of his sisters' romance novels. Despite the fact that her boyfriend did not appear to be terribly handsome, Geraldine seemed enraptured by his company. One fact was clear to Sean. "Frankenstein" obviously possessed some intangible quality that Sean felt deep down he didn't possess. Was it charm – was it charisma? Was it an extrovert nature or just a lack of shyness? As the pair kissed, Sean looked away as he just found it too upsetting to watch. He was pleased to see Kevin and his blonde companion Fiona getting on well. Kevin came across to some people who didn't know him terribly well as a little lippy and arrogant. But Sean knew that, deep down, he had a good nature and that, despite the misfortune he had to bear with the premature demise of his father, he never felt sorry for himself and had the dignity to keep his grief private.

"With all the people I know,

I'm still a lonely man.

You know – it's funny.

I thought I had her in the palm of my hand."

The words of the song summarised exactly how Sean felt. As he looked around the hall, watching so many people he knew, laughing, singing, dancing and enjoying each other's company, he felt so lonely inside. Moreover – it was a profound loneliness – totally unlike any feelings of loneliness he had experienced as a child without any brothers. This was loneliness on a totally different level. He closed his eyes, hoping that it would go away.

As the end of "Have you Seen Her" gave way to the beautiful opening bars of Elton Johns "Your Song"; Sean, who was fond of the song, reflected upon the lyrics, wondering whether it was possible to be as blissfully in love with another person as the songwriter implied. He was sure that his father and mother loved each other, but his father would never express his love in such gushing, sentimental terms. He doubted very much that the songwriter was a rural, Irish catholic, or if he was, he was untypical of the breed. Maybe the song was some skilfully created, romantic illusion – written solely to make money, rather than human emotions put to pen as a consequence of direct personal experience. "How wonderful life is – when you're in the world." He particularly pondered upon this lyric. He thought about his mother's eldest sister, Josephine. She was a nun and had spent some time in Africa. She was always happy and smiling and yet she had no "special" person in her life. Perhaps some people were more dependant than others for companionship. Sean certainly couldn't envisage life in the priesthood as a route to blissful happiness. He also intended to travel when he got older – to experience life and to learn from people who were not so influenced by the philosophy and ways of Irish Catholicism.

Kevin and Fiona were by now looking very much like boyfriend and girlfriend. As the song drew to a close, they both made their way to the exit, presumably for a bit of 'courting'. Sean had the sofa all to himself. Gemma, Fiona's friend; having finished dancing with Noel McCanny, came over and sat beside him. "You look in a bit of a bad mood," she remarked to Sean. "Ach no – I'm just a bit sleepy." "It's past yer bed-time then?" "Maybe – I see your mate has gone out with my mate." "Aye – she has a funny taste in men has Fiona." "Kevin's all-right - he just takes a bit of gettin'ta know." "What about you – do you take a bit of getting'ta know?" "What do ye mean?" inquired Sean. "Well – ye don't seem to be just as extrovert as yer mate." "I'd probably be a bit more introspective than him." "What were ye introspectin' about a minute ago – dreamin' about bein' the real Marc Bolan?". "Well – I was just thinkin' about what I was goin' t'do with meself when I get older," retorted Sean, who wasn't about to confess his feelings about Geraldine Donnelly to a girl he hardly knew. "And have ye any definite plans?" "Maybe travel a bit – what about yerself?" "Well – me elder sister's a nurse over in London. She trained up in the Royal – but when she qualified she wanted to get out of Belfast. I might give the nursin' a go meself." Gemma and Sean continued their conversation. Suddenly – as the lights came on The D.J. said, "Well – that's another Hallowee'n night over. Take care on the way home everyone – and remember – there's no such thing as ghosts! "

"I better go look for Fiona here – her da's pickin' us up," said Gemma as she got up from her seat. "Gemma!" replied Sean, as he reached under the sofa for the rubber snake. "Do ye want to take Gloria out with ye?" "Not on yer life!" giggled Gemma. Sean went looking for his two sisters. He met Siobhan, who had just returned from the cloakroom with her coat. "Where's Mary, Siobhan?" "She's gone out wi' big Shuggy." "Who?" "Big Shuggy – ye probably don't know him. He plays football for Cuchullains." "Can't say I do." "Me and you'll go down and wait for daddy – she won't be long." Sean went back to retrieve his "guitar" from under the sofa. As he and Siobhan made their way out, he met Geraldine Donnelly on the way on to the cloakroom. He had momentarily forgotten about Geraldine and couldn't help being captivated by how beautiful she was. She was wearing a low-cut suede dress, which revealed a little cleavage. He'd rather not have met her at all. She bade Siobhan and Sean goodnight in her usual pleasant, friendly manner. Sean and Siobhan bade her likewise. Mary caught up with her younger brother and sister a few minutes later just before Peter arrived to take his children home.

CHAPTER 8

Christmas Eve 1972.

School had closed for a fortnight three days ago and the pre-Christmas tests were over for another year. Sean thought that he had done O.K. overall, though he was convinced he had failed Latin, with Irish being a possible borderline case also. He had postponed buying his new guitar and amplifier until the New Year as his mother had advised that a few pounds could be saved by waiting for the January sales . Kevin was by now going out with Fiona, but had been seen kissing another girl from the convent under the mistletoe at the bus-station on the last day of term. His sister Mary had told him that Fiona had found out about it and was angry. Mary had also told him that she had heard that Gemma was showing a bit of interest in him. Sean didn't know how to react to this. He was flattered but would rather hide the fact from Gemma that he was shy and inexperienced with girls. He thought about what he would do if he met her at a disco over Christmas.

Sean's parents had gone into town to do some shopping and he had gone over to his Uncle Gerrys to help feed the cattle. Darkness was falling on the cold, crisp, clear evening and Sean could see and smell the cattle's warm breath as he and Patsy broke the bale of hay for them to eat. It was eerily quiet. "Remember the two fellas who were done in not far from here 'round Hallowe'en time," said Patsy. "Aye – down near Newtoncutler wasn't it – they called it the Pitchfork Murders on the news." "I heard me ma and da talkin' about it. They were talkin' to friends of theirs about it who live 'round there and they said that the stuff about the pitchforks was all made up – they were supposed to have been stabbed to death by the Brits." "Are ye sure Patsy – would the Brits not just have shot them and said they were runnin' away or somethin'. I think it was the UVF that did it." "The folk that live there say the Brits were 'round that house that evenin'". "Jesus – you're givin' me the willies Patsy – the Brits could be watchin' us from that hedge right now!" "They're everywhere those bastards. Scumbags from the backstreets of Glasgow and Liverpool sent over here to put the Paddies in their place." The silence was broken by the monotonous, distant drone of a helicopter. "Even on Christmas Eve - some things never change," said Sean. "I always pity the fellas in jail in Long Kesh at this time o' year," said Patsy. "Some o' them aren't much older than you and me y'know." "I know – and those are the best years of their lives – or should be. Ye're only a teenager once."

When they had finished feeding the cattle, Patsy and Sean fed meal to the young calves, which were kept inside. The cosy, straw-filled pen reminded Sean of the crib in the chapel. "Sean and Patsy – I've a bowl of hot soup ready for ye both. Come on in while it's still hot." "Comin' now ma," shouted Patsy. Sean's Aunt Kathleen had used one of the legs of the Christmas turkey to make a large pot of soup. He reckoned it was the most delicious bowl of soup he had ever tasted, but modesty prevented him from asking for a second helping. "Do any of ye want anymore?" "Aye – OK aunt Kathleen. That's great soup," remarked Sean. "The turkey-leg makes great soup – and there's always too much turkey left over in this house after Christmas dinner. I think I'll do this every year from now on, especially as me wee nephew likes it so much." "We couldn't do that in our house. The turkey leg is the only bit of the turkey that Granda would eat," replied Sean. "Where's da gone Ma?" inquired Patsy as his mother gave him a second helping from the ladle. "He's gone into town for his wee Christmas drink wi' Hughie Scullion. Maybe you could do the milkin' for him at half-six if he's not back out again Patsy. He only goes for a drink two or three times a year." "Are ye goin' to stay and help me?" Patsy inquired of his cousin. "May as well." "Come on inta the sittin' room – we'll take the soup and watch TV for half-an-hour".

CHAPTER 9

Christmas Day 1972.

Christmas Day, as in many other households, was a special day for the Daly family. The children bought presents for their parents and vice versa. Sean always gave money to his two sisters, who took care of the present-buying. This year the girls had bought their daddy a new watch as he had damaged his old one at work. They also bought a bottle of perfume for their mother and a packet of War Horse tobacco for Granda. The year before, they made the innocent mistake of buying another brand, which had caused him to be less than happy, so they were careful this year not to repeat their mistake.

"Sean – come down to the spare room till I show ye somethin'," said Brigid. Sean followed his mother down to the spare room. Peter and the girls, both of whom were curious, followed. On the chair there was a quadrangular cardboard box about three feet six inches high. Sean knew instantly what it was as he picked at the sellotape to open the box. It was an acoustic guitar. He lifted it out of the cover and looked it up and down before smelling the delicious scent of quality wood emanating from the sound-hole. "Aw ma,da – thank ye both so much – I couldn't have picked a better present meself." "We were goin' to get ye an electric one but the fella in the shop says ye're better learnin' on the ordinary one – it makes yer fingers strong-er," remarked Peter. "There's a book there too Sean and the wee thing ye pick it with," said Siobhan. The book was called "A Tune a Day For Guitar", but Sean was so taken with his new present that he barely noticed the book. He lifted the plectrum and strummed the strings lightly. "The fella tuned it for us in the shop and he said changes in tem-perature could put it out a bit," added Brigid. "I'll have to get a few lessons somewhere," said Sean. "Hey Sean – once ye learn to play - we could start a wee group," joked Mary. "You and Siobhan will have to practise yer harmonies first pet," laughed Brigid. "By the way – you girls have to come into the kitchen to help me with the Christmas dinner." Sean – you can come into Mass with me – the girls and yer mammy went to Midnight last night," said Peter. "Ok Da" replied Sean. Given the choice – he would have preferred to acquaint himself with his new instrument. Still – it would be tempting fate not to show some gratitude to the Al-mighty for such an excellent Christmas present.

The Christmas Mass was probably the only Mass in the year which Sean found in any way meaningful. It was the combination of the excellent choir, the lifesize crib and the celebration of the birth of Jesus which made it a spiritually uplifting event. He wondered what Christmas was like in Communist countries like Russia or China. As he looked around him watching old and young, working-class and middle-class, families and single people praying together – he felt glad to be part of the global Christian community.

When they arrived home from Mass, Brigid and her two daughters had preparations well underway for the Christmas dinner. The turkey had been cooking since 6am and the aroma permeated the kitchen and beyond. Sean and his father helped set the table with the silver cutlery Peter and Brigid had received many years ago as a wedding present. After completing this, Sean went to the spare room to spend a bit of time fiddling about with his new present. It would be a long time before he would be able to say to someone that he "played" the guitar. He flicked through the pages of the tuition book and noted that the tunes seemed to be written in musical notation. This was something he didn't understand and he made a resolution to himself that in 1973 he would unravel the mysteries of written music.

At half-past-two Brigid called everyone into the kitchen. Granda sat at one end of the table; Peter at the other. Set in front of each person was a meal fit for a king - freshly cooked turkey, boiled ham, carrots, brussel sprouts, boiled and roast potatoes and cranberry sauce. There was no wine to drink as everyone with the exception of Granda was teetotal. Granda himself didn't drink wine – only Powers Whisky or bottles of Guinness. Instead the drink of choice was apple-juice.

"Thank God it wasn't a white Christmas," said Peter. "Aye – I mind the winter of '47 – there must've been two-feet of snow 'round here that year," replied Granda. "What did ye do at Christmas when ye were younger, Granda," enquired Mary. "Well – there used te' be cockfightin' on near here on Boxin' Day. A friend of mine, Big Pat O'Neill, used to keep game-cocks and we'd take them t'fight. Sometimes ye could make a few bob – other times ye could lose a few bob." "God Granda – cockfightin'. That's cruel - I didn't think you'd be at that," replied Mary. "Maybe – but if them' oul cocks dandered by one another in the farm-yard - ye can be sure they'd lay inta one another without anybody havin' ta tell them," said Granda. "But they put steel spurs on their feet at the cockfights, Granda," replied Sean. "That they do, but at least the cocks have a chance to live to fight another day. This turkey we're ea-tin' didn't have any chance of makin' it past Christmas." "But in cockfights the birds are killed for sport – not for eatin'," said Siobhan. "Well - ye have ta remember that in them days there were no TV nor swimmin' pools or what have ye. People made their own sport - trainin'n' handling game-cocks was a skill handed down from father ta son. Big Pat could have sucked the blood out of a hurt cock's neck faster'n anyone I ever seen." "Hi Granda," said Brig-id. "Could we turn the conversation back to the big winter of '47. If ye go inta any more detail about what ye're talkin' about – I don't think I'll be able to finish me dinner."

There was much laughter. Sean, who enjoyed listening to Granda's moral defence of the practice of cockfighting, resumed eating his dinner. He had heard about the big winter of 1947 more times than he'd cared to remember. When the main meal was finished and Brigid and the girls were busy clearing up, Sean decided he would find out a bit more about his Granda's hitherto hidden past as an assistant cockfighter. "Did ye ever referee a cockfight yerself, Granda?" "Naw son – I wasn't really inta the cockfightin' the way Big Pat was. I never rared any birds of me own or anythin'. I just enjoyed the craic with the men that were there. We'd all go for a drink after." "Did anybody ever get arrested by the R.U.C.?" inquired Peter. "Naw – the R.U.C. turned a blind eye. There was nothin' political about it. Some of the R.U.C. men were probably cockfightin' men themselves." "It's died out 'round here though," said Peter. "Aye – it has. There's still a bit o' cockfightin' goes on 'round South Armagh though." "The gypsies are big cockfightin, men," said Peter. "Oh aye – some gypsies used to come to the cockfights 'round here. They always had plenty of money 'n Big Pat said that their birds were always tough and hard't'beat." "Just like their owners – the gypsies are big inta bareknuckle boxin', and all that." "Did ye ever see a bareknuckle boxin' match Granda?" asked Sean excitedly. "I saw two gypsies fightin' bareknuckle at a horsefair in Monaghan town when I was a young fella. Both of them were bate blackn'blue but after an hour one of them gave in. He couldn't stand up any more." "Was there money ridin' on it Granda?" "Oh Aye – they were from two different families and there was a lot of money ridin' on it. But the boys themselves was fightin' for pride. There's a lot of bad blood between some o' them gypsy families." "Guess we better tune the conversation back to the big winter of '47 again,"muttered Peter. "Here comes dessert."

CHAPTER 10

23rd January 1973.

It was a cold, rainy Tuesday night. Brigid had gone to a game of bingo and the girls were in their bedroom studying. Granda, Peter and Sean were in the sitting-room in eager anticipation of a heavyweight boxing match, the coverage of which had just commenced on T.V. Moreover – this was a new colour T.V., which Peter had bought a fortnight before, in the January sales. For the past two weeks Sean had even been watching programs, like the soap opera Crossroads, which he wouldn't normally have watched. Some of the actresses on the program, whom he previously hadn't noticed when the old black-and-white TV was in the house, suddenly had become quite good looking.

Joe Frazier, the world heavyweight champion, was defending his title against a young heavyweight called George Foreman, who was relatively unknown despite having won the gold medal at heavyweight for the U.S.A. amateur team at the Mexico Olympics in 1968. All three generations of the male side of the Daly family had an interest in boxing. Sean and Peter's interest was mainly stimulated by the media coverage of the ex-champion Muhammad Ali, whereas Granda belonged to an earlier generation of fight-fans who had grown up listening to boxing on the radio back in the days when a lot of the top fighters such as Gene Tunney and Jimmy McLarnin were of Irish parentage.

As the two fighters warmed up in their corners, Peter asked his father, "who's goin' to win this one?" "I don't know anythin' about the other fella but that Frazier is a tough, hard man. He's one of the few about the day who could have fought in the 30's and 40's." "Frazier's never been beaten – has he Sean?" asked Peter. "Not as a professional anyway. Mind ye – I don't think Foreman's been beaten either." "Should make for a good fight then." The two fighters met in the centre of the ring. Foreman – who was a few inches taller than Frazier, was staring at the champion intently, a menacing scowl etched on his face. "God – look at the size of that big fella. His head's takin' up half the TV screen," exclaimed Granda. "I hope Frazier dosen't have a childish accident before the fight starts. It must be a wee bit un-nervin' havin' a big brute eyeball ye like that," remarked Peter. "Maybe Foreman's more scared than Frazier is," replied Sean.

The bell went. The fight was on. The three viewers watched in silence as the two black fighters stalked each other, each looking for an opening. "Frazier's tryin' to set Foreman up for the left hook," said Peter. "He's just after missin' with one there," observed Sean. Foreman shrugged Frazier away from him and planted a couple of solid left jabs in the champion's face. Seconds later – a thunderous uppercut from the challenger left the champion on his knees. "Holy God," exclaimed Granda – "I don't believe it." Frazier got up right away but he was obviously quite shaken by the punch. He signalled to the referee that he was fit to continue, but shortly after, another powerful uppercut landed flush on his chin and put him on the seat of his pants again. "This is like the 1st Liston-Patterson fight," remarked Peter. "The challenger is beatin' the champ up and the 1st round isn't even over yet!" Unfortunately for Frazier it wasn't and he was knocked down a 3rd time before the bell signalled the end of round one.

"That big fella is a human wreckin' ball!" exclaimed Granda. "I've never seen anyone hit that hard." "D'ye think Frazier will recover before the next round and find his rhythm again?" asked Sean. "It's hard to see. Foreman looks like a man on a mission," replied Peter. The second round continued in much the same pattern. Foreman steered Frazier into a corner and continued his battering-ram assault. When Frazier tried to nip out of the corner – a clubbing right-hander to the side of his ear put him down for a 4th time. "Frazier ye eejit – why don't ye take advantage of the count instead of gettin' up right away all the time," muttered Granda. "He's like a badger caught in the headlights of a speedin' car – just waitin' for the impact," replied Peter. Seconds later Frazier was down again for a fifth time. "The ref's gonna have te stop it soon," said Sean. "Frazier can't take much more of that. It dosen't matter how tough he is." Sean's observation came true a few seconds later. The sixth and final knockdown was a punch which seemed to lift Frazier momentarily off his feet. The referee stepped in and signalled to Frazier that it was all over.

"Foreman could be the champion for years to come. He's only in his early twenties," stated Peter. "I wonder will Ali and him fight now," inquired Sean. "That big lump 'll eat the pretty boy up for breakfast," replied Granda. "It's hard to know – Ali has a style better suited to fightin' big, powerful men like Foreman. Remember what he did to Sonny Liston," observed Peter. "I think they'll fight sometime. Ali wants the belt back and nobody other than him has a chance of beatin' Foreman," said Sean. "They'll both make a fortune out of it," noted Peter. "I hope I'm alive to see it," said Granda.

CHAPTER 11

Wednesday 14th February 1973.

Sean was up early that morning. Although he wasn't by habit an early riser he had a reason for being up before anyone else. This was Valentine's Day and he was curious to see if he had received any Valentine cards in the morning post. He was also intent on getting any cards out of his parents' way in case there were any naughty rhymes written on the cover. Sure enough there was a pink envelope with his name and address on the front. He slipped it under his pyjama top and took it back to his bedroom. The envelope had a scent of perfume and on the envelope seal were inscribed the letters S.W.A.L.K. Sean wondered who the loving kisser was who had sealed the envelope. He took out the card and proceeded to read the verses, looking for clues.

"Roses are red – violets are blue. Hell is hot – and so are you."

The handwriting was large and rounded. He hadn't seen it before.

"My hair colour is black – My teeth shining white. I've a pert little bottom. It's quite warming cold nights."

"Black hair," mused Sean. "Could it be Gemma?"

"I'm really quite fit. Neither skinny nor fat, And can be quite charming. Liking this – liking that."

This bit interested him, as he never found skinny girls or plump girls aroused him much. Gemma was neither skinny nor fat. Maybe it was her who sent it?

The poem ended with "To add to all this I have something to rhyme. I love you – will you Be my Valentine."

There were a few other little ditties written but they didn't yield any clues as to who the sender was. As his mother would be tidying the room later, he put the Valentine card inside his chemistry book. He would read it again when he came home in the evening after school.

At break-time that morning, after a double period of Art; Sean, Patsy, Kevin and some of their classmates were talking about what they had received in the post earlier. "I never got anything," admitted Patsy. "I got two," replied Noel McCanny. Sean thought that it was probable that Noel didn't get any Valentine cards, but there was no way of disproving him. "I got one in a pink envelope. Thank God me ma didn't see it," said Sean. "Did it say who it was from Sean?" inquired Kevin. "It might be Gemma – your girlfriend's mate. She said she had black hair and wasn't skinny or fat." "Might be. Fiona dosen't love me any more though." "Did ye fall out?" "Somebody told her I was kissin' somebody under the mistletoe. She took the hump and blew me out." "No Valentine cards for you then, loverboy," joked Patsy to Kevin. "Naw – I did get somethin' else though." " What d'ye mean?" asked Noel. "D'ye want t'see. I have them in me schoolbag", replied Kevin. Kevins use of the word 'them' had aroused the curiosity of his classmates to a degree whereby, if he had charged them all twenty-pence each to see inside his schoolbag, they most likely would have paid him. As he opened the schoolbag he explained, "I had te take this to school. Me ma would've stood over me this evenin' and made me open it in front of her. Once I felt the soft feel of the envelope – I knew damn well somebody was up ta somethin'."

Kevin took out the contents of the envelope. It was a pair of underpants decorated in small red hearts. There were hoots of laughter all around. "I'm surprised ye're not wearin' them Kevin. They're so fresh and clean," laughed Patsy. "Any idea who sent them?" asked Noel. "Damn the one – there was no writin' or card or anythin'. Somebody's messin' with me mind big-time. The address on the front is written in capitals."

The bell for the end of break-time sounded and the boys went back to their class. At dinner-break the boys were in the table-tennis hall. They were discussing what to do with Kevin's Valentine "present". "What about puttin' them onto that dummy that they use to display the school-uniform for the open night tonight," suggested Noel. "That's an idea," replied Patsy. "Will we put it on over the trousers or take the trousers off it?" "Aye – we'll take the trousers off it and put on these things instead just before we leave school. Some of us 'll have to keep an eye out for the teachers though," replied Kevin. "I'll keep dick," offered Noel. At 3.30 the four boys went down to the small store-room at the back of the assembly hall. The room had a back-exit, which could be used as an escape route in case a teacher came into the hall to access the store-room. Sean checked the back-exit door to ensure it wasn't locked. Noel kept an eye on the assembly hall exit and Patsy and Kevin set about removing the trousers of the display dummy. "These things won't come off past the feet," spoke Patsy in a hushed tone. "Hurry up for God's sake!" urged Noel. "This thing's on tonight. Somebody might come down any minute to move it into the hall!" Noel's thought-provoking comment caused a collective adrenalin surge on the part of the practical-joke conspirators. "Here - use my pen-knife to cut the trouser-legs off at the bottom," whispered Sean. Patsy took the knife and cut the bottom of each leg of the trousers while Kevin ripped them from the dummy as Sean held it. "McCanny – put them trousers in that plastic bag there – we'll dump them on the way home," instructed Kevin. "No trousers – no crime," whispered Patsy as he sniggered.

"Now for phase two," laughed Kevin as he took the decorated underpants from his schoolbag. "Jesus – quick boys! The Goat and Jimmy Blink are after comin' thru the door –they're headin' down this way. Hurry up fer God's sake!" whispered an agitated Noel. The four knew there would be Hell to pay if they were caught: not only from the headmaster, but also from their own parents. "That's them on now boys," whispered Kevin triumphantly. "Come on – let's get out of here!" The four grabbed their schoolbags and made their way to the bus-station via the back-exit door just seconds before the two elderly teachers entered the room. As it turned out, Mr Mc'Closkey and Mr Mc'Donald had both been asked by the vice-principal to assist with getting the assembly-hall ready for Open-Night. The former had been given the moniker "The Goat" because of his thin face and unkempt facial hair. The latter had developed a habit of constantly shutting his eyelids, hence his nickname. As Mr Mc'Donald entered the store-room, Mr Mc'Cluskey bent down to tie his shoelaces. "Edward – come in here and take a look at this!" exclaimed Mr Mc'Donald. "God Almighty – someone's removed the trousers off the display dummy." "And replaced them with something else. A pair of spotty knickers no less." "Maybe they were on it already – underneath the trousers I mean." "I doubt it Edward. We're going to have to find a replacement pair of trousers before half-seven!" "I think we better let the head know about this. I get the feeling he won't be terribly happy." "You do that. I'll get a measuring tape and get the size. The uniform-shop in the town shuts about five. We've got time to get a replacement set." Five minutes later there was a knock on the headmasters office door. "Yes – come in," spoke a small, dark, bespectacled priest. "Fr McGuigan – I ah – think ye better take a look at this." "What is it Edward – I'm busy trying to get the loose ends tied up before tonight's function." "Somebody has removed the trousers off the uniform display dummy." "WHAT – DID YOU SEE WHO IT WAS?" The headmaster – a wiry, intense, hyperactive man, was up on his feet immediately. "There'll be hell to pay for this Edward if I catch the perpetrators!" "That's not all Father – they've replaced them with something else." "My Goodness – we do have some sick minds at this school. What have they replaced the trousers with?" "A pair of red, spotty underpants, Father." "RED, SPOTTY UNDERPANTS – I REALLY DO NOT BELIEVE I AM HEARING THIS!" "I think ye better come and have a look Father – Jimmy has gone into town to get a replacement pair in the shop before it closes." The irate headmaster left his office and proceeded in the direction of the storeroom at a speed which would have done justice to an Olympic 50km walking champion. Mr McCloskey struggled to keep up with him before deciding it was pointless. Thus the headmaster's initial reaction upon seeing the bizarrely dressed dummy was not noted by any of his underlings.

The next day at assembly hall – an agitated Fr Mc'Guigan gave a stern lecture to all the boys who stood before him. A few little glances were exchanged between some boys in the third form near the back of the hall. Needless to say – the perpetrators did not suffer from any pangs of conscience, and no subsequent admissions of guilt were forthcoming.

Chapter 12

April 1973.

It was the week after Easter. The weather was warm, the sun was shining and the dark, wet days of January and February seemed a distant memory. Sean was on holidays from school that week and in no hurry to get back. Peter and a couple of his colleagues were doing some maintenance work in the area that week and he and his two co-workers had been taking their lunchbreak at the Daly's home. One of the workers was a young, long-haired fellow called Mickey Donaghy. He was twenty-one years old. Sean was busy learning some chords on his guitar in the adjoining room, the door to which was open. Mickey walked in and sat on the seat next to him as he was practising."Your da was tellin' me you're teachin' yerself to play, Sean" said Mickey. "Well – I'm tryin'. It's takin' me ages to get from one chord to the next," replied Sean."I can show ye a couple of things if ye want," said Mickey. Sean handed Mickey the guitar. "This is the wee lick at the start of the rock'n'roll tune 'Shakin' all Over'.""Ye pull off the top string with the 3rd finger at the 3rd fret. Nearly the same on the 2nd string, except ye don't pull off. Go from A to G on the 3rd string with the big finger and then E-D-E on the 4th string. I'll play it for ye a couple of times slow and you can try it." Mickey played the lick three times slowly then a few times at normal speed. "This is the wee lick on the bottom strings just after it.

Ye need to use the fleshy bit at the side of yer hand to damp the strings for the right effect." Sean was mightily impressed by the way Mickey had played the lick. "Now – try it to see if ye can get it." "I'd love to learn that – it sounds better than ploddin' away at chords all the time." "If ye want to improve – it's important to play stuff that ye like. Otherwise ye'll eventually get bored." Sean tried the lick as Mickey had taught him. "Don't forget to damp the bottom strings with the heel of the hand," reminded Mickey. "Hi Mickey – time to go back to work," reminded Peter. If ye get that lick right by Friday – I'll lend ye some records to listen to," said Mickey, as he put on his coat.

For the rest of the afternoon, Sean rarely put the guitar down. The tips of his fingers became red and raw. But he willingly absorbed the pain. More than anything he want-ed to impress Mickey and pass the test which had been set for him. The next day Mickey showed him how to play the opening chords of the song "All Right Now" by the rock-band Free. "It's just two chords – A and D. Ye just have to make yer change quick and clean." "I'll never be able to get from A to D that quick. It'll take me years." "Ye'll be surprised y'know." "Do you play in a band?" inquired Sean "I play lead guitar in a wee country band at weekends. It's not really the music I want to play but it's not a bad way of makin' a few extra bob", answered Mickey. "Would ye not like to play in a band full-time?" asked Sean. "Aye – but me da's not well and me ma needs me about to help her look after him. Me older brother's married 'n livin' in England. I'm the breadwinner." "What sort of guitar d'ye play?" asked Sean "It's a Fender Telecaster. Me brother's a guitar-player too and he gave it to me before he went over the water." "What sort of amp do ye play it through?" "A Fender Twin Reverb – it's a heavy brute, but it's got that clean twangy sound that ye need to get the right tone for country-style lead guitar." "Some day I'm goin' to get an electric guitar like the one Marc Bolan has," remarked Sean. "That's a Gibson Les Paul. They're a great guitar for playin' blues because they have a thick, woody tone but they're very dear. Ye'd be better buyin' a Japanese copy of a Les Paul." "What's blues Mickey?" asked Sean. "Ye'll find out about the blues come Friday. If I start talkin' about the blues – they'll never get me back to work," said Mickey as he reached for his donkey-jacket. As Mickey left, Sean pondered upon what he had just said. Obviously this "blues" was something which Mickey felt passionate about. Although he had only known Mickey a couple of days – he could see that, despite the age difference, they were in a way kindred spirits. He knew already that Friday was going to be an important day in his life. On Thursday Sean practised everything that Mickey had taught him. Mickey and Peter weren't there that day, but on Friday Mickey arrived for lunchbreak at Daly's with a plastic bag under his arm. Sean knew that these were the records Mickey had been talking about but thought that he had better let him eat his lunch first before peppering him with questions. Fifteen minutes later Mickey walked into the room where Sean was practising away. "I see ye've been puttin' the work in so I brought ye these to listen to," said Mickey. He took the three records out of the bag. "I take

it ye have a record-player." "Aye – it's in the girls room."
"Be careful and don't scratch these Sean. This one is Jimi
Hendrix's first album – Are You Experienced. This one is a
live album by the Rolling Stones called Get yer YaYa's Out
and this one is Bluesbreakers by John Mayall." "I've heard
of the Rolling Stones allright and I think I've heard of Jimi
Hendrix. The other fella I haven't heard of," replied Sean.
"He's the leader of an English blues band. Eric Clapton
played on this album." "Aye – that name's familiar." "This
album was made back in 1966. Clapton played a Les Paul
through a Marshall amp. His playin' is so clean and fluid.
You won't believe the sound he gets." "What about the
other two records?" "The announcer at the start of this
Stones album calls them the greatest rock'n'roll band in
the world and you only have to listen to this to see that
he's right. Every song is a classic. The styles of the two gui-
tar-players mesh so well as they play so differently. Keith
Richards with his rugged, tight rhythm playin' and Mick
Taylor, who only joined the band three months before this
was recorded., plays every bit as good as Clapton. I spend
a lotta time playin' guitar with this album – listenin' for
licks and chord-changes and tryin' to copy them." "Is that
not hard to do?" inquired Sean. "At the start it is. But once
ye get the chords of the song – ye can work out the licks.
Ye have to know yer blues and pentatonic scales." "Sounds
like I have a lot to learn. What about this fella Hendrix?"
"Well Hendrix died back in 1970 – but he's the greatest
electric guitar-player that ever was and ever will be. He's
a bit of a hero of mine. This was his first album – made in

1967 when everythin' was psychedelic. He wrote and sang all the songs as well as doin' all the guitar work on them. My favourite song on this is the one called Red House – on side 1." "Why is it your favourite?" "Because it must be the greatest four minutes of electric blues guitar that's ever been put on record. Hendrix learned from listenin' to old Chicago blues records before he took the blues in his own direction. But this is him returnin' to his roots. I think that's the only song on the album that he didn't use a Fender Strat.." "Can you play any of it?" "I can play the lick at the start and some bits in the middle, but nobody could play it as well as he does. The man was a bloody genius. It's a shame he died so young. That fella on the front – Noel Redding. He's a Corkman – believe it or not. He's the bass-player."

"Hey Mickey - are ye comin'. Payday's this afternoon," called Peter from the next room. "Aww God – back to dreary reality," sighed Mickey. "Thanks a lot for these albums. I'll take good care of them," retorted Sean. In his haste to catch up with the two older men, Mickey bumped into Mary on the way out, nearly knocking her down. "Sorry love," he apologised. "I didn't see ye." Sean, who saw it happen, expected his sister to be angry. But instead she was blushing – something he had never seen her do before. "I'm all right. Ye better hurry or ye'll miss yer lift," she replied.

CHAPTER 13

Friday 4th May 1973.

It was a sunny Friday evening. Patsy, Kevin and Sean; who all played for the Tir-na-Nog Under-sixteen Gaelic football team; were getting ready to run to the pitch. Their opponents were Cuchullains and the match was for a place in the final of the Under -16 Championship.

The two teams were pretty evenly matched. The year before they had played each other to a draw. That match had been a keenly contested affair and in his pre-match pep-talk, the team manager was reminding his charges how the opposition on that occasion had come close to winning the game."Don't let that big bastard in the middle of the field run the show the way he did the last time boys. Mc'Peake – you try and catch him with one of yer wee left hooks to the back of the kidneys when the ref. isn't lookin". Pat "Jabber" Mc'Peake nodded silently. Jabber wasn't the quickest or most skilful player on the Tir-Na-Nog team. But he had advanced through puberty, was sporting a black moustache and had a certain ruthless quality that, combined with his heavy build, tended to create an aura of fear among his opponents. In underage football some players still had to go through the stages of puberty and it was hard not to be intimidated by someone from the opposing team who looked mature enough to be your daddy's drinking partner. "Jabber" hadn't played in the drawn match and the look on his face implied that he knew he had a job to do and he had every intention of doing it. Sean was playing at right half-forward. Patsy was playing at left half-forward and Kevin was playing at full-forward. Kevin wasn't the best catcher of a ball but his speed and eye for a goal combined with his soccer skills made him a handful for opponents to mark. "Hi Sean – play it in for me low," said Kevin as they ran out onto the pitch. "I'm crap at catchin' the high ball."

The ref. threw in the ball and the match was underway. Sean knew a couple of the Cuchullains players. Their centre half-forward was Fergus Quinn – one of the best footballers in their school. Quinn had a left foot which was incredible in its accuracy. He could find players in space with pinpoint passes and make it look easy. He was also a superb dead-ball kicker and their manager had warned them not to give away too many soft frees as Quinn would punish them. Sean hoped that Quinn was going to have an off-night. He also recognised the big midfielder who had given his team a hard time in the previous encounter. His team-mates called him P.J. Another top Cuchullains player, their full-forward Phonsie Kelly had been off school all week and wasn't playing tonight. His place had been taken by a pudgy, overweight youth, who Sean didn't recognise. At least the Tir-Na-Nog full- back was going to have an easier time tonight, he thought. Suddenly a miskicked ball came Seans way. He managed to grab it. Sean lacked the pace necessary to outsprint defenders and his policy was to pass as soon as possible to a better-placed team-mate. He followed Kevin's pre-match instruction and shot in a low ball. As Kevin sprinted out to meet it, his marker, who was a burly fellow with ginger hair, vigorously pursued him. As Kevin grabbed the ball, the defender shoulder-charged him with all his might and knocked him to the ground."Well played, Shuggy," shouted the Cuchullains manager from the sidelines. "Don't give him any space." Sean recalled the name from the Hallowee'n disco the year before. He wondered if his sister was still romantically linked to the ape-like defender. The referee ruled that the charge was fair. Kevin, obviously affected by the force of the challenge, got to his feet after a few seconds but didn't complain. Five minutes later a high ball from midfield by PJ was caught cleanly by the fat youth in the Cuchullains forward line. Demonstrating a nimbleness of foot beyond anyone's expectations, he neatly sidestepped his marker, before chipping the ball delicately in the roof of the Tir-Na-Nog net. There were roars and cheers from the Cuchullains supporters. "WAYYE BOY PORKER – BRILLIANT!" shouted the Cuchullains manager, as he waved his clenched fist in passionate approval. Despite his team being on the receiving end, Sean thought it was one of the best goals he had ever seen. Perhaps he had underestimated "Porker". Even Phonsie Kelly would have been proud of that goal. Stung by the fact that they were three points down so early on in the game, the Tir-Na-Nog players came back strongly but the Cuchullains backline defended resolutely. It was nearly ten minutes later before Patsy, with a surging run from his own half laid on a perfectly placed pass to the left corner-forward who sent the ball over the bar from a sharp angle. Shortly after that, in what was nearly a carbon-copy of the earlier goal, PJ sent another high ball in the direction of "Porker". It was a little too high to catch but Porker still managed to jump and thump it with his fist. The Cuchullains defenders looked on as the ball sailed over the bar for a point. The Cuchullains manager was ecstatic, an emotion not shared by his counterpart. "PAT!" shouted the Tir-Na-Nog manager, pointing at P.J. "PAT!" he shouted again, gesticulating with his forehead to "Jabber". A couple more points were exchanged on either side. Both were frees. Fergus Quinn scored one from thirty yards out and Kevin kept Tir-Na-Nog in touch with a free at the other end, the referee judging on that occasion that Shuggy had fouled him. About five minutes from half-time another high ball came into the midfield. Four or five players went up for it – among them PJ, who was taller then everybody else. Sean, who was about ten yards away from the action, heard a high-pitched squeal as the ball went through P.J.'s hands to be picked up by one of Sean's team-mates who kicked the ball back up the field. PJ was on the ground, holding his back. As nobody had saw anything, play was waved on. Jabber was running backwards, keeping his eye on the game. Fergus Quinn went over to PJ and signalled for the referee to blow the whistle. As the ball had gone out of play, he did just that. PJ was helped off the field and shortly after the whistle blew again for half-time.

The Tir-Na-Nog players gathered around their manager for the half-time pep-talk. "Right boys – things aren't goin' our way – but it could be worse. Two things we need to do. Tighten up the markin' on the fat full-forward.Ye're givin' him too much space Padraig. Second thing we need to do is get a goal. Jabber – when you win the ball don't boot it up the field. Pass it to Patsy and let him pick out the forwards in space. And for God's sake don't give away too many frees. Quinn hardly ever misses."

When the players came out for the second–half, Sean noted that PJ still looked a little the worse for wear after his "accident" in the first-half. Tir-Na-Nog were three points behind however and the Cuchullains defence was proving a hard nut to crack. Still, if Jabber did as he was told and gave the ball to Patsy, whose passing skills were almost as good as Fergus Quinn's, things might open up for them. As the referee threw in the ball for the second-half, Jabber palmed the ball down to Patsy who played a quick fisted pass to a team-mate before running into space. He received the ball back and went on a solo run up the left-hand side of the pitch. One of the Cuchullains defenders shoulder-charged him but bounced off him. He was looking for Kevin, who came running out to meet him to receive a short, fisted pass. Kevin played it right back to Patsy as Shuggy was just behind him.He received the pass and sent in a low hard shot with his favoured left foot. The goalkeeper dived in vain as the ball sailed into the back of the net. The Tir-Na-Nog Supporters, including Gerry and Peter, were delirious with joy. Patsy shook his fist in the air.

Sean was delighted, as much for the fact that it was Patsy who scored the equaliser as anything else. Fergus Quinn might be some player, but he wasn't half the player his cousin was. How could they lose with a player like that in their team? The Tir-Na-Nog manager was shouting, "That's it boys – keep goin' at them. Keep the momentum." And Tir-Na-Nog did keep the momentum. Encouraged by the superb score taken by their best player, the mediocre players in the team, including Sean, raised their game. Within the next 15 minutes they were three points up. Noel McCanny, playing on top of the right, scored the point which put them in front. Kevin scored a second from a free and Jabber even got in on the act by scoring a point. Cuchullains didn't give up easily, but their first-half tactic of pumping the ball in high to the full-forward was no longer proving effective. P.J. was no longer dominating the midfield, with the consequence that the game was slipping away from them. The Tir-Na-Nog manager kept exhorting his players to greater effort, well aware that the tide of the game could turn in an instant.

But in truth the game was won ten minutes before the final whistle. Jabber fisted another ball to Patsy about forty yards out. He took careful aim with his left foot. The ball rose high in the air before curving down sweetly between the posts. Nobody had expected Patsy to try for a score so far out. But Patsy was no ordinary player. Cuchullains scored another point before the final whistle. When the referee blew to signal the end of the game – the Tir-Na-Nog supporters ran onto the field. The final score on the scoreboard read Tir-Na-Nog 1-6 - Cuchullains 1-3. They had made it to the final! The players on both sides shook hands after a hard, tight game. Fergus Quinn shook hands with Patsy and congratulated him. The two players had a great mutual respect for each other's ability and played together on the school team. "I prefer playin' with ye than agin ye," said Quinn. "Me too", said Patsy. "Who's the fat fella?" "Oh ye mean Porker. He can play a bit – can't he." The Tir-Na-Nog manager came over to shake Patsy's hand and the two players bade their farewell. "Boy did ye turn it on for us in the second-half! That's one of the best games I've ever seen ye play!" Patsy smiled. As the sun set over the hills of Co Tyrone and the smell of freshly mown grass lingered in the air, Patsy savoured the moment. This was what he lived for – and it really couldn't get any better.

CHAPTER 14

Saturday 5th May 1973.

Sean awoke the next morning a little later than usual. He was a bit stiff and was suffering from a "dead leg", having taken a knock late in the game. But Tir-Na-Nog were in the final and the discomfort was a small price to pay. His mother and father had already gone into town to do the shopping. "Do ye want scrambled egg on toast Sean?" inquired Siobhan from the kitchen. |"Aye – I'd love some. I'm takin' a quick bath here t'ease me aches and pains. We won last night y'know." "Aye – we heard. This'll be ready for ye in 15 minutes." Twenty minutes later Sean hobbled into the kitchen and took his seat at the table. "Did ye get any scores last night Sean?" asked Mary. "Naw I didn't. Patsy scored a goal and a point." "Good for him. What about Kevin – did he score?" "Only one point from a free. That big boyfriend of yours was markin' him." "Who – aw ye mean Shuggy. He's me ex-boyfriend. We finished at Easter." "If he'd come to the fancy-dress last Hallowe'en as one of the Flintstones, wearin' a goatskin and carryin' a club – Kevin would have been in second place" remarked Sean. Siobhan giggled, but Mary was angry. "That's not fair Sean.-comparin' Shuggy to a caveman. He bought me a ring when we finished." "Did he finish with you?" "No – I finished with him." "If he was so nice – why did ye finish with him?" "Well – I sort've got bored. Ye can only talk so much about Gaelic football and snooker and Shuggy didn't talk about anything else," explained Mary. "Us girls need a wee bit of intellectual stimulation, Sean" interjected Siobhan. "Did he talk about any of the players on our team?" "Well – I used to switch off when he started talkin' about Gaelic. The only one I remember him talkin' about was Patsy. He said Patsy was a class player." "He won the game for us last night. Ye should have seen that point he scored at the end." "Well – I hope ye's win the final," replied Mary.

"Sean – Mary wants t'know somethin'", said Siobhan. "About what?" replied Sean. "Shut up Siobhan!" Siobhan was enjoying the effect her teasing was having on her older sister. Sean was puzzled. "What do ye want t'know, Mary?" "Nothin'." "She wants to know if that fella that works with daddy is comin' back to show ye any more guitar tricks." "I was not!" responded Mary angrily. "Don't listen to her." Sean remembered how Mary had blushed when Mickey had accidentally bumped into her. On second thoughts, maybe it wasn't an accident. Perhaps Mary had got herself in his way on purpose. But his big sister had always helped him out and lent him money when he needed it. He wasn't going to tease her. "Why don't ye listen to those three records he lent me. And ask him some intellectually stimulatin' questions. Oh- don't forget te tell him you're a big Jimi Hendrix fan," advised Sean. Siobhan giggled. "God Mary – did ye know that men are capable of being intellectually stimulated. I didn't think that was possible." "Funny enough – I've already been listenin' to them. The Hendrix one's my favorite of the three." "Well – I don't know when he'll be back. But he'll be lookin' the records back and I'll tell him you've been listenin' t'them."

"Aw look – she's all pleased Sean." Siobhan gave her sister a hug. "Time to head over to Patsys for a chat about the match. Are ye's watchin' Leeds and Sunderland in the FA Cup final today?" inquired Sean. "Ah no – we have to go shoppin'," replied Mary. "No intellectual stimulation to-day then," answered Sean.

CHAPTER 15

Wednesday 9th May 1973

Mary heard the telephone ring around 7pm and took the call. Occasionally some of her classmates would ring and they would discuss homework questions. This time it was a male voice at the other end of the line. "Could I speak to Sean please?" "He's actually over at his cousins at the minute. Can I leave a message for him?" "Aye well – its Mickey Donaghy here. I left three records with him a few weeks ago - could ye ask him if it's alright to collect them again this weekend?" Mary's heartbeat quickened a little. "Oh aye you're the fella ……." She cleared her throat. "Aye I'll tell him. Actually, I've been listenin' to them meself the last week or two. Ye don't have any more Hendrix albums – that was the one of the three I liked the best." "I can lend ye Axis Bold As Love if ye want." Mickey spoke the album title so quickly it sounded like one word. "Axesboldas? What's it again?" asked Mary. Mickey laughed. " I'll just bring it down to ye on Saturday. Are you the sister I bumped inta that last day I was down?" "That's me." "Spose I owe ye a favour then. Night." "Night now," uttered Mary as she put the telephone back on the receiver. Her heart was fluttering and it was a few seconds before she regained her composure.

"Who was that?" inquired Siobhan. "It was Mickey, the fella that works with daddy – he's comin' down this Saturday to lift his records and he's bringin' me down another one." "Well you're obviously excited about this. I'll have ta get a proper look at this fella," replied Siobhan."He's got lovely brown eyes and sort of tanned skin," said Mary blissfully. "What age is he?" "I don't know – I'd say about twenty." "Well if he's twenty and good-lookin' he might have a girlfriend y'know. Just be cool until ye find out the score," advised Siobhan.

On Saturday afternoon a battered yellow Ford Escort pulled up at the front door of the Daly household. The driver got out, switched off the engine and rang the door-bell. Mary, who had been anticipating the visit and had spent some time in front of the mirror making herself look nice, answered the door. "Hello", said Mickey. "I forgot t'ask ye yer name on the phone the other night." "Mary - you're Mickey," she replied. "Y'must be the only female Hendrix fan I know," he said, handing her a copy of Axis Bold As Love. "Thanks. He's not me No1 favorite – but I liked that record y'lent me brother." "Who's yer No1 favorite." "Marc Bolan." "He alright, but he's not a patch on Jimi. That album; if y'liked the first one – ye'll like it too." "What's the best song on it?" "I think the best one is Little Wing. It's a slower tune but there's beautiful guitarplayin' on it." "Well – I'll listen t'that one first," replied Mary. Peter, who had recognised Mickey's car, spoke in a loud voice. "Mary – are ye bringin' that man in for a cup of tea. He's been workin' hard all week y'know." The pair smiled at each other as Mary opened the door into the living-room, letting Mickey in first."

"How are ye Peter – not often I see you sittin' in a chair takin' it easy." "Just rechargin' the batteries. I see the wee motor is still goin'." "Just about. She was in the garage gettin' the clutch fixed this week. What about the Beetle – is she still goin' allright?" "Goin' well," replied Peter.

Mickey and Peter chatted, while Brigid and the two girls made the tea. Mary put the three records in a plastic bag and handed them to Mickey."Where's the guitar player at the day?" inquired Mickey. "He's over at his cousins house. The two of them have a big football match comin' up soon and they're out every weekend practisin'. He told me t'thank ye very much for the records though," replied Mary. "I didn't know Sean played Gaelic. Is he any good?" "He OK and he tries hard," replied Peter. "His cousin Patsy would be better than him though." "Ah well – ye can't be good at everything."" Did you play football Mickey?" inquired a starry-eyed Siobhan. "I think me and Sean have a lot in common. I tried but I just didn't have the right build or that real will-to-win thing." "That's probably the thing ye need more than anythin'," said Peter. "That young nephew of mine - Patsy. He's an easy goin' boy - but when he goes onto the pitch - he's like a different person." "Like Dr Jekyll – Mr Hyde," remarked Mickey. "Sort of. Mind ye – he's not a dirty player. It's just a real determination that ye're either born with or not. He's got no fear and even if the team are getting' beat – he never gives up. Yet when he's off the field – he's so laid back nothin' bothers him." "Except the British Army," noted Siobhan. "Are ye playin' out anywhere tonight Mickey?" asked Brigid. "Aye

- we've a gig at a pub near Stuartston. After that we're takin' a few weeks off. The other two boys in the band are farmers and they'll be busy." "What do ye do on yer time off?" inquired Mary. "Well fixin' the car is one thing. Mind ye – there's a rock-band comin' to Ardhoe dancehall next week. The Dirty Harries – they play the heavy stuff. I'll want to see them." "What's that name again?" asked Brigid. Everybody laughed - especially Peter. "The Dirty Harries Brigid. I'm surprised ye haven't heard of them." "Would ye take me t'see them?" said Mary excitedly. Before Mickey could answer, her mother interjected, "You're only sixteen dear – you're too young t'be goin' to dances!" "But I'll be seventeen in a few weeks mammy - my friends are allowed t'go te dances. Why can't I go?" Peter, spotting that Mickey was uncomfortable at being the unwitting cause of a family argument, diffused the situation. "Mary love - yer mammy and me 'll have a wee chat later. Mickey might already have plans to take somebody else y'know." "Naw – I haven't Peter. I'll give her a lift surely. But only with your permission." Mickey glanced at his watch. "Hi – I'd better be on me way. Tonight's my turn for doin' the drivin'. Thanks very much for the tea Mrs Daly." "Anytime son – you're always welcome here." Mickey lifted the plastic bag and made his way to the door.

When Mickey had left – an emotional Mary made her way out of the sitting room. Before she left she said to her mother, "Mammy – why do ye make me look like a wee silly girl all the time!" Her sister Siobhan followed her. Brigid looked at her husband with tears in her eyes. "I'm not tryin' to spoil her fun Peter – I worry about her." "I know love. But she'll be seventeen soon and she's a sensible girl for her age. And I know young Mickey well from work. He's a good lad and responsible as well. I think we'll let her go." "D'ye think so? Maybe you're right." "You'll alienate her if ye keep treatin' her like a kid. At least with Mickey she'll be safe. He dosen't drink y'know." Brigid, who was a member of the Pioneer and Total Abstinence Association, was relieved to hear this. "Well – he is a likeable young fella." "Right – I'll let you tell her she can go." "I s'pose Id better tell her right away," retorted Brigid.

Chapter 16

Saturday 19th May 1973.

Mickey arrived at Daly's house around half past eight in the evening, Peter having told him during the week that it was O.K. for Mary to go to the dance with him. Mary, who was dressed in denims with a white blouse, answered the door. "Mary – you're dressed to kill t'night." "So are you – are ye comin' in a minute t'say hello. I have t'get me bag and jacket." Peter and Brigid greeted Mickey as Mary hugged both her parents and said good bye to Sean, Siobhan and Granda. "Ah Mickey – try not t'be too late", requested Peter. "We'll leave right after it's over," replied Mickey. As the car pulled out of the driveway, Brigid was unable to resist looking out of the window as the tail-lights of the Ford Escort disappeared into the distance. "There goes my wee girl," she muttered to herself.

Mary wasn't looking out of the back window however. She knew that the days of going to youth-club discos were now a thing of the past, as she looked forward to a new and exciting phase of her life. "I had to tidy up the car a bit for ye,"said Mickey. "Well – you done a good job. I hope we don't get any flat wheels tonight. Daddy had one last week." "Can I ask ye a question?" "What is it?" replied Mary. "Do ye have a boyfriend?" "No – I'm a single girl. I was going out with a fella for a few months, but we finished at Easter." "Ye look older than seventeen. Or ye seem more mature than seventeen." "Well – I won't be seventeen until June. What age are you?" "I was twenty-one in April." "And do ye have a girlfriend?" "Naw – I was goin'out with a girl when I was nineteen. She was killed in a bomb." "Oh God – I didn't know. Jesus – that must have been terrible for you." "Well – I admit I still think about her but I haven't been to see her family for a year now. I'm still young – I have te move on with me life." Mary – not wishing to intrude on Mickey's private feelings or wishing to trivialise the matter by changing the subject, felt unsure of what to say. After a moment, Mickey said to her "Give me your hand." She reached her hand to him. "Like I said – what's past is past - we're goin' to enjoy ourselves tonight." He squeezed her hand gently. She squeezed his hand gently. They held hands for a few seconds. "Time for a gearchange," said Mickey jokingly as they broke hand contact. The journey took over an hour, during which time Mary and Mickey talked about school, parents, relationships and music. Mickey wasn't particularly interested in football but Mary didn't mind that. She found him interesting to talk to. He had left school at sixteen, but was obviously intelligent. Conversation ebbed and flowed naturally between them and even having to queue at an Army checkpoint did not cause either of them undue annoyance as they found it so easy to be in each other's company.

By the time they arrived at the dancehall, it was still too early to go in. "Fancy a burger?" asked Mickey. "Aye – but not too many onions," replied Mary. "I might be a minute or two – there's a queue at the chipvan." "Don't worry – I won't be runnin' off anywhere," laughed Mary. As Mickey went off to buy two burgers, Mary surveyed her surroundings from the top corner of the large carpark. As she watched the showband's large van pull in and park next the back door of the hall, she was thinking about the conversation Mickey and herself had together, particularly when he asked her if she had a girlfriend. Was he interested in her romantically or was he just making polite conversation? Though she found him very attractive, perhaps it would be a good idea to remember her sister Siobhan's advice about playing it cool. After all – she didn't know him terribly well and she didn't want to appear over-eager to be his romantic conquest. Fifteen minutes later Mickey arrived with two steaming hot burgers. "I hope these are worth the wait," he said. "I think I'll let mine cool down a bit first," replied Mary. "The band only arrived when you were away queueing." "They won't be on stage for another hour then," replied Mickey. "I s'pose these boys would have a bit more equipment than your wee band." "Aye – they'd have big Marshall stacks and they're a five-piece with a keyboard player – we wouldn't have half as much stuff as them." "Your band is just bass, guitar and drums isn't it. Who does the singin'?" The bass player mostly - I do vocal harmonies with him on some tunes. But I'm not the worlds best singer." Mary laughed. "You've got me curiosity workin' overtime now. Siobhan and meself are gonna have to come and see ye's play sometime." "Maybe – mind ye the stuff we play is American country music of the 1950's with a bit of Irish folk music stuff. We're not exactly cuttin' edge prog. rock y'know." "I don't mind that. Besides – there's something homely and appealin' about an old-fashioned man. Ye's don't wear woolly jumpers like Val Doonican do ye's?" joked Mary. "Finish eatin' that burger before it goes cold. Our bass player 'll be here tonight. I'm gonna tell him you've been makin' fun of our wee band," replied Mickey. He was enjoying the banter. "Oh – I hope he's not a sensitive sort. Some people can't take a slaggin' too well." "Sensitive isn't the first word that comes t'mind when I think about him." "Well – what is the first word that comes to mind?" "It's hard to put into words. But if ye meet him tonight – ye'll know what I mean," replied Mickey. "I see there's a queue formin' at the door. S'pose we may as well join it." "I'm glad I've me jeans on tonight – it's too cold for a skirt," remarked Mary, as she finished off her burger and got out of the car.

Mickey locked the car doors and the pair made their way down the hill to join the back of the queue. "By the way – I've money t'pay meself in," whispered Mary. "No way – you're my guest. I'm payin' us both in. Ye can buy me a lemonade though. That burger's left me thirsty." It was quite dark inside the large hall and there were still relatively few people inside. Mary went off to get Mickeys lemonade and a coke for herself. She looked around, hoping to see someone who looked around the same age as herself. She didn't know anybody. Having purchased two bottles, she made her way over to the far side of the hall where Mickey was seated. "Your lemonade sir," she proffered. "Thank you m'dear," he replied. They sat and chatted while the band set up the final pieces of equipment before proceeding to run a soundcheck. The loudness of the amplification took Mary by surprise. "God – what's it goin' t'be like when the whole band get goin'." "Your ears'll be used to it and the hall'l be full of people by then. "No sign of your bass player yet." "Not yet – him and the drummer'll probably come together along with the drummers young brother."

Forty minutes later the band, without any prior introductions, launched straight into the opening chords of the Black Sabbath song Paranoid. As they did so, the doors of the hall swung open like a scene from a wild-west saloon and three young men raced up the hall to about ten yards from the stage One of them was a short, squat fellow with a baldish head who was wearing a white shirt. The other was a lean, lithe youth with long dark hair dressed in faded denims. The third was a muscular, athletic fellow dressed in darker denims with long, fair hair. They were all obviously in the prime of youth with energy to burn. The two long-haired fellows stood about six feet apart and began shaking their heads with their long, flowing locks to and fro to the two-chord rhythm of the heavy metal classic, while playing imaginary "air" guitar. The short, squat fellow was doing a hopalong type dance between his two companions, while also playing an imaginary guitar. "DUH,DUH,DUH,DUH,DUH,DUH,DUH,DUH,DUH,DUH,DUH,DUH,DUH,DUH,DUH,DUH, – DUH,DUH,DUH,DUH,DUH,DUH,DUH,DUH, BAM BAM BAMP"

The thunderous, repetitive guitar riff backed with the bass and drums filled the hall as more people started to spill in the doors. Attempting to have a conversation in these circumstances was pointless, thought Mary. She momentarily forgot about Mickey as she looked on; fascinated with the size of the hall, the loudness of the music and the enthusiastic gyrations of the three male "dancers". It was as though she were being transported back in time to some sort of stone-age ritual. She noticed that Mickey was holding his hand over his face, obviously very amused by the three "headbangers". He seemed to be trying not to laugh too hard. The lead singer was screaming out the lyrics with all the gusto at his disposal, grabbing the microphone-stand as if his life depended on it. Then – halfway through the song came the vocal break for the guitar solo. The three left their original position to continue their activity at the feet of the lead guitarist who stood near the front of the stage. Mary couldn't help laughing - she was laughing at Mickey laughing as well as at the antics of the "headbangers". She wondered how their ears and neck muscles would feel the next day, having been subjected to such high volume and rigorous exertions.When the song was over, Mary turned to Mickey and remarked, "This is good fun – Will we join these three out on the floor?" "I think ye'd be crampin, their style. I take it ye don't know who they are?" "No – I've never seen them." "The one with very little hair – he's the bass player I told ye about. The well-built fella's our drummer and the other fella's his brother. He does roadie for us sometimes." "Oh God – if they see ye – they'll want ye up there with them!" "Aye – but if you sit on me knee for a while till the crowd comes in – they'll not notice I'm here." Mary didn't need to be asked twice and perched herself up on Mickey's knee. "Ye can't leave a young thing like me alone in a big hall like this Mickey Donaghy!" laughed Mary as she put her right arm around his neck. Mickey laughed. He enjoyed Mary's natural, unaffected outgoing personality. He studied her flawless skin and fine facial bone structure. He felt the warmth of her body and noted her fragrant smell. One or two beautiful girls he had known had high opinions of themselves and a pretentious manner but Mary was not at all like that. Moreover, he had a lot of respect for her father who had gone out of his way to make him feel one of the team when he had started working for the Electricity Board. He looked at her long, slim legs and couldn't help wondering what she would look like in a short skirt. He had to admit to himself that he was growing fonder of her by the minute. He put his arms around her slim waist as the first song drew to an abrupt close. The three "headbangers" held their clenched fists in the air, giving the band their verdict of approval.

Mary, taking advantage of the momentary drop in the decibel level, asked Mickey if he did any headbanging in his spare time. "A bit – but I prefer to watch." The lead singer introduced the next song. "This is a song by Led Zeppelin from 1969 – it's called Whole Lotta Love." "Shane'll go mad for this one – it's his favourite song of all time," said Mickey enthusiastically. "Which one's Shane?" inquired Mary. "That's the drummer – the big fella," shouted Mick-

ey back in her ear. "BA-BA-BABAM BAMP". Shane raised
his two fists in the air as though he had scored the winning
goal in a cup-final. By now more "headbangers" had joined
them at the front, swinging their long locks to the beat of
the mesmerising Jimmy Page guitar riff. "That's the music
at the start of Top of the Pops," shouted Mary. "Aye – it's
the same tune", replied Mickey."Will we go for a walk – see
if we know anybody?" said Mary as she nodded her head.
"Down this way – not up near the front," replied Mickey,
pointing with his finger. Mickey took her hand and the pair
walked together around the hall. Mary bumped into one
of her classmates, Maire O'Loan. They were friends and
delighted to see each other, but the loud music made any
sort of prolonged conversation difficult. Mary introduced
her friend to Mickey, aware that no doubt she would have a
couple of questions from her classmate on Monday at break-
time. After a minute they were continuing on their way,
hand in hand as before. Mary asked Mickey if the band
played any music in the pop charts. "I think they play Thin
Lizzy's Whiskey in the Jar." "If they play it – can we go out
and dance?" "If ye want – I s'pose that's why we came."
About ten minutes later the band broke into Whiskey in the
Jar. Mary tugged Mickey and they made their way out onto
the dancefloor. The two shook their bodies whilst clapping
hands and singing the lyrics. When the chorus line came
they locked arms and spun each other around. Mary was
having the time of her life and Mickey, though a bit more
reserved, was enjoying himself also. They stayed up for the
next couple of songs until the band called a short break.

As they were walking over to the side, Mickey's three friends were making their way down to the bottom of the hall. Jim McKenna the bass player spotted Mickey first and pointed him out to Shane and Colm Nolan. "Hi boys – look who's here!" recognising Mickeys rear profile. "The bastard never told us he had a girlfriend," replied Shane. "She looks allright from the back - come on and we'll say hello 'n see what this woman looks like from the front," said Colm. "Hi - he's gone to the toilet. Come on an' we'll wind this wee girl up a bit – tell her a few fibs before he comes back out again." The Nolan brothers laughed and followed behind Jim as he went up to Mary and tapped her on the shoulder. "Hello love. You don't know me – but there's somethin' ye should know about yer new boyfriend." "He's not my boyfriend -what is there to know anyway?" replied Mary, pretending she didn't know who McKenna was. "Well – sometimes he asks girls out just to be seen with them. But he's really gay – he dosen't fancy women at all!" "Are you sure ye aren't gay yerself? Ye remind me a bit of that fella on TV – Larry Grayson," responded Mary sarcastically The two brothers really cracked up at this as McKenna did bear a faint resemblance to Larry Grayson. Just then Mickey emerged from the toilet. "Hello boys – I see ye've already met Mary. What have ye been tellin' her about me." "Jim's been singin' yer praises Mickey," laughed Shane as he put his arm on Mickeys shoulder. "I'm sure he has – good band the night eh!" replied Mickey. "F------g brilliant - hi mate are you and the new woman comin' out for a freak-out in the second-half," inquired Jim. "Well

– this girls daddy wants her home early. We might leave before the end for it's a good hour's drive." "Aw Jesus mate – ye're getting' old before yer time", replied McKenna. "Shane – where's that half-bottle. We'll go inta the bog for a swig before the band comes out. Colm - you're drivin' mate. You can't have any." "Don't remind me Jim," replied the younger Nolan. As the two went off to the toilet to imbibe some hard liquor, Jim reminded Mary. "Don't forget what I told ye love." Mary laughed. Mickey asked Colm what the two were drinking. "They had a few beer on the way up. Some oul' boy – a neighbour of Jim's, gave him a half-bottle of poteen. He sneaked it in with him." "He'll be in bother if the bouncers catch him," remarked Mickey. "Jim would tell them its water and he'd make such a good show of it they'd probably believe him," laughed Colm. Mickey and Mary laughed. Just then the band returned to the stage. "Hi – Mickey. I'll see ye around. Nice meetin' ye Mary." "You too Colm," replied Mary. When Colm had gone out of earshot, Mary remarked, "they're a lively bunch them friends of yours." "Aye they are - ye wouldn't describe Jim as shy and sensitive would ye?"" Naw. I like Colm - he's a nice fella." "Aye Colm's the best – what was Jim sayin' when I was in the toilet?" "Nothin' much – he just wanted to know if I was your girlfriend," laughed Mary with a twinkle in her eye. "Is that all? – Jim would spin ye a yarn very quick y'know." "I was only talkin' to him for a second," Mary replied.

Their conversation was interrupted by what seemed to be a disturbance at the far end of the hall. People were standing on the wooden seating and craning their necks in order to get a better view of what was happening. Mickey stood up on the seat to have a look. "What's happenin' over there Mickey?" inquired Mary. "There's a fight broken out - the doormen are involved in it too." "Are your friends in it?" "That's what I'm lookin' for but I don't think they are." As more people ran over to the far end of the hall to get a better view or become personally involved, Mickey said, "I think this might have somethin' to do with a football match last weekend between Na Fianna and Pearses. A fella got his nose broken in the match and I saw a couple of his brothers here earlier. They're two hard men." "Oh Mickey – don't you be gettin' involved in it!" "I've no intention of it. Unless the bouncers get it under control quickly it's goin' t'get out of hand." "Maybe we better leave early Mickey. God knows what'll happen." "Well – I better get you home safe. Yer da wouldn't be happy if I let anythin' happen to ye. Wait at the door and I'll get me coat." Two minutes later the pair walked out together into the brisk, clear, moonlit night. "It's a beautiful night. I can smell the summer comin'," muttered Mary as she grabbed Mickeys arm. "Y'know – years from now we'll think back on these days as the best of our lives. We just don't realise it now," replied Mickey. "You're quite the philosopher," purred Mary in his ear as she huddled close to him. "I won't be so philosophical if this car dosen't start." "Ah don't worry. Ye could ring daddy up at that phone box over there and he'd come and collect us." Mickey got into the front seat and turned the key in the ignition. The engine responded favourably. "Looks like we won't need yer daddy after all," said Mickey as he drove slowly to the carpark exit.

During the return journey Mary talked to Mickey about his three friends. Mickey was telling her about how Jim was an enthusiastic practical joker who took delight in playing all sorts of tricks on people. "There was one night Shane got himself a lovely blonde at a pub we were playin'. She was a university student or somethin'. When Shane went off to the toilet, Jim told her that Shane had a wife and kid. When Shane came out again the woman had disappeared. Big ladies-man Shane couldn't figure out why this woman had left without even a goodbye." "Is Shane a bit of a ladies man?" inquired Mary. "That's about the only night I ever saw Shane have a problem with a woman." "What about you – are you a ladies man?" "Not really – I s'pose I'm quieter than Shane. Most of the women ye meet in the places we play are older anyway. They're usually married or with boyfriends." "And Shane snaps up any loose ones." "That's about it," retorted Mickey. "You're not gay are ye?" inquired Mary. "What! Do I look gay?" responded Mickey, somewhat taken aback by the question. "Jim told me ye were gay earlier when ye went off to the toilet." "Bastard – I'm goin' to have t'get him back for that," answered Mickey. Mary didn't believe that Mickey was gay, but decided it would be fun to pretend that she believed Jim's remark. "Y'know Mickey – there's nothin' t'be ashamed of about bein' gay. There's more gay men out there than you think an' they're not all effeminate in the way they act and look." "But I'm not gay Mary! Jim's only windin' ye up and because ye're young ye believe him! What exactly did the wee bastard say to ye?" This was the first time Mary had seen Mickey riled and she was laughing to herself. "He says ye only go out with women t'be seen with them." "God – I'll get even with the wee runt if it's the last thing I do!" "Mickey – it dosen't bother me personally if ye're gay or not. I'm a girl who can keep a secret. Ye'll feel a lot better if ye tell some-one ye know." Mickey was becoming angry. He spotted a picnic-area sign fifty yards in the distance and indicated to turn in. "Where are ye goin'?" asked Mary. "We left good'n early didn't we," responded Mickey emphatically. "Aye – so." Mickey pulled the car into the picnic-area and turned off the engine. He adjusted the lever on the front passengers-seat pushing the backrest back to a horizontal position. He grabbed Mary by her shoulders and pushed her down on the seat. Then he lay on top of her. "Mickey Donaghy – what are ye doin'!" "I told ye twice I wasn't gay but ye're still not convinced. I think I'm goin' t'have no op-tion but t'prove it to ye." Before she could reply he kissed her hard on the lips. For a second she made a futile effort to resist. He already had his arms around her. She opened her mouth and wrapped her arms around his lean, athletic frame. He slid his hand under her blouse and rubbed it up and down her bare back. Their tongues met and they kissed each other passionately. After about three minutes Mickey broke off. "Now - d'ye still think I'm bloody gay!" Mary stroked his face with her hand and smiled. "I'm still not convinced. Ye might have t'do that again." He smiled back at her. "I suppose I just might," he replied.

CHAPTER 17

Saturday 9th June 1973.

Sean, Patsy, Peter and Gerry were on their way to a bog deep in the heart of the Sperrin Mountains. They were going to spend the day cutting and spreading turf. The two grown men did most of the cutting. One would cut for an hour whilst the other would throw the turf slabs out onto the bank for the two boys to build on the turf barrow. Gerry and Peter were joint owners of the bog, and the turf-cutting every year was usually done on the first good weekend day in June. Sean and Patsy had been brought along by their fathers since they were nine or ten years of age. Whilst the work was repetitive, it wasn't nearly as physically strenuous as potato gathering. Gerry and Peter also let their two sons do some cutting as they wanted the pair of them to acquire the skills which would prove useful in the years to come. A lot of the rural Irish Catholic families managed to get by on a tight budget and one of the principal means of doing this was by stocking up with plenty of turf to reduce the winter heating bill. In fact both of the Daly families had to buy very little coal. Gerry had a small trailer attached to the towbar of his Hillman Hunter. He pulled the car up at the entrance gate to the bog. A couple of other cars were there also. Gerry took the turf-barrow out of the trailer and gave Patsy the turf spade. Sean took the lunch and Thermos flask and Peter took the other spades, which were used for paring the bank. It was about a mile walk to where the Daly's bog was located.

One of the things which Sean liked about the annual turf-cutting expeditions was that one was always liable to bump into a host of interesting characters. Unlike potato-gathering; which was performed by people his own age whom he met on an everyday basis or harvesting the hay, which was a family affair; turf-cutting was an activity which was pursued by a variety of folk in proximity to each other. Some of the bogs near to the Daly bog were rented out to different people. Other families, like the Dalys, cut their own turf.

One character whom they had met a couple of times in previous years had been nicknamed "Bean-Si Johnny" by Patsy. He was an eccentric rustic in his seventies who lived somewhere near the Tyrone-Derry border. He was intensely superstitious and seemed to have a habit of bringing the conversation around to the subject of Bean-Si's. He would then tell a story of an up-close-and-personal encounter he had with a Bean-Si, when he was a young man coming home from a ceilidh one dark night. He told them the same story two years in a row but in the second version he was coming from a wake rather than a ceilidh. Patsy found this amusing and hence coined the nickname. "D'ye think Bean-Si Johnny 'll be here this year?" said Patsy to no one in particular. Peter laughed. "He's a funny oul' boy that. Ye never know – he could be here all right."

Fifteen minutes later the foursome had arrived at the Daly's turf bank. It was a bright sunny morning, but there was always a strong breeze on the mountain. Sean had suffered some painful sunburn the previous year and had brought a tube of suncream with him this year. He also kept his shirtsleeves down. Patsy buried the two bottles of water in the slushy turf at the bottom of the bank to keep them cool. Before they could start digging, the sods at the top of the bank would have to be pared. After a minute they were ready to start. Gerry stood facing the bank and began slicing four-inch thick grassy sods. His movements were fluid and rhythmic with little wasted energy. Up on top of the bank, Peter was nicking the sods into square-foot sizes. When he had one nicked all the way around, Gerry would lever it out with his spade and the two boys would carry them down to behind Gerry where they would be laid out on the ground for building in later. This job took over half an hour. When it was completed they stopped for a quick drink of water. Gerry then lifted the turf-spade. He nestled his right boot comfortably in the lug of the spade, and started to dig. As before – his movement was fluid and rhythmic. Peter tossed the wet, brown turf up onto the top of the bank, whereupon the two boys built them onto the barrow. Sean liked the smell of the freshly cut turf. In fact he loved everything about the bog. He loved the fresh air, warm sun, panoramic view and wide, open space. It was a place where he felt at one with nature, with blood-relations whom he had known all his life. It was a place far away from life's petty worries such as exam results, school and girlfriend problems. Patsy wheeled the barrow a good thirty yards before tossing the contents onto the side of the grassy hill. Sean spread the turf out to let the sun commence the drying process. Patsy was talking about the match, which had been postponed due to the death of a club member of the opposing team. "It might be three weeks before the final's played y'know," said Patsy. "I hope none of our boys are away on holidays at the time," replied Sean. "God forbid –them Wolfe Tones are a good team. We'll need everybody," retorted Patsy. "There's a couple of them goin' to the Gaeltacht in Donegal but I think they don't go till August." "Even if they were – they could always come back for a day. This is a one-off thing. Unless ye've another year left ye won't get the chance again. I wish the game was on tomorra. I can't wait," remarked Patsy as the two boys strolled back to the bank to put on another load. When the barrow was full, Sean took his turn to wheel. He wheeled the barrow up to where Patsy had dumped the first load, before emptying its contents.

And so the Daly turf-cutting team toiled on until half-past-one. After working steadily for over three hours, the two cousins were famished. They used some of the bottled water to wash their hands and dried them by rubbing them on the grass. Sean reached for the Thermos flask and proceeded to pour four cups of tea. Patsy distributed the milk and sugar. Peter handed everyone a roast beef sandwich and the four sat down to enjoy a well-earned rest.

About ten minutes later a man passed by near them. He waved at the Daly team and they waved back. He sauntered down onto the Dalys bank. "Peter – Gerry. Are ye's well. Hello boys." "Not so bad Tom. It's a good dryin' day today eh," replied Gerry. "Aye – the turf wouldn't be long a dryin' with a few days like that." "Is this yer first day up," inquired Peter. "Naw – I was up earlier in the week. I'm turnin' mine the day." "Has oul' Johnny been up yet this year," asked Gerry, who knew that Tom was a neighbour of Johnny's. "Johnny died about six months ago Gerry - ye didn't hear?" "Agh – I didn't know that. What happened him?" "Well he had heart problems for a long time – Johnny lived on his own y'know 'n I s'pose he didn't take great care of himself. He was on tablets but he told me once that he used to wash them down with poteen." "Jesus," exclaimed Patsy. "That couldn't have been good for him!" Despite the sad news, Peter couldn't suppress a smile. "He was a character oul' Johnny – wasn't he," re-marked Peter. "I s'pose ye heard his yarns about the bean-si," replied Tom. "Every year – he could tell a good story oul' Johnny. What age was he anyway?" inquired Peter. "He was seventy-two. Are these two boys football men?" inquired Tom. "Oh aye – they're playin' in the Under-16 final in a few weeks time. The match was put off," replied Gerry. "I'll have ta go and see that. With all this walkin' up and down turf banks ye's 'll be the fittest men on the field," joked Tom. "Well – I s'pose we better get back to it before the rain comes on," replied Peter, having noted that the sun had disappeared. "I'll see ye's later – best of luck in the big game boys". The two boys thanked Tom and the four made their way back to the bank. "Do any of youse two boys want to dig for a while?" asked Gerry. "I will", replied Patsy.

Nearly four hours later, Peter looked at his brother. All around them were sods of turf, drying in the sun. "Think that'll do us the day Gerry," he said. "Aye – we'll come back next week and turn them." "Will we head home boys – or do ye's want to work on another while?" shouted Peter; smiling to himself as he knew what the response would be. "All right da – Patsy and me 'll just finish off here," replied Sean.

CHAPTER 18

Wednesday 13th June 1973

Peter and his two workmates in the Electricity Board were on their lunchbreak. They had been working all morning, putting a pole in the private garden of a house about half a mile outside Killacran, a small Protestant village. Mickey wasn't with them as he was away on a training course. Peter's two colleagues on that occasion were Protestant men. Wesley Adams was an older man, about Peter's age. Peter and he had known each other since the mid-1960's. Mervyn Black was a younger man in his mid-twenties, who had only joined the Electric Board a couple of months previously. Peter didn't really know him though he seemed a friendly enough sort of fellow. The three were sitting on a grass verge on the other side of the house, eating their lunch in the glorious summer sunshine. A motorcycle pulled up alongside the men. Both the rider and pillion passenger were wearing helmets. The pillion passenger dismounted from the bike and pulled a Browning 9mm pistol from a shoulder holster inside his jacket. He was only six feet from Peter. Peter suddenly realised, to his absolute horror, that the gunman was about to shoot him. But he barely had time to move before the gunman opened fire and shot him in the head. The gunman walked over to Peter's outstretched body and fired a second shot to the head, fatally wounding him. The gunman put the gun back in the holster and remounted the motorbike. The motorbike sped off, back in the direction from whence it had came. "Mervyn – go into that house and ring 999 for an ambulance!" shouted Wesley. As Mervyn sped towards the house, and dark blood seeped from the head of Peter's prostrate body, Wesley checked for any sign that his colleague was still living. Peter wasn't breathing and there was no sign of any pulse. By the time Mervyn had come back out of the house with the lady owner, Wesley had already put his coat over Peter's lifeless body. As the woman put her hands over her face in horror, Wesley said to her, "It's not the ambulance we need – it's the police. He's been murdered!"

Around 2pm, Sean was sitting in Geography class, taking notes from the teacher. It was a lovely sunny day and he was sitting by the window. The subject matter for today's lesson was English coalmines. This was an aspect of geography which held no interest for him. He was looking out of the window, daydreaming about the upcoming summer holidays. There was a knock on the door. The school secretary entered. "Mr Grimes, - the headmaster wishes to speak to Sean Daly in his office." "Sean, - could you go with the secretary." Sean arose from his chair. He was trying to think if he had done anything wrong. Could it be something about the uniform display dummy? He reasoned otherwise as some of his classmates would have been called with him. Out in the quiet corridor, Sean noticed that the secretary looked a little upset. Her name was Annie Quinn and she was a neighbour of theirs, though he didn't know her terribly well. "Are ye all right Annie?" inquired Sean. "I'm all right Sean," she replied as a tear trickled down her face. She touched him lightly on the shoulder with her hand before walking ahead of him.

Later, that evening, a BBC TV presenter for the local news programme Scene Around Six read out the headlines. "A workman has been shot dead near the Co Tyrone village of Killacran. A motorcycle drew up as the man and his colleagues were having lunch and the pillion passenger shot the man, a 49 year-old Catholic, twice in the head, killing him instantly. The loyalist paramilitary group, the U.V.F., have claimed responsibility for the murder, stating that the dead man was a member of the I.R.A.. Both the police and the dead man's family have strongly denied the allegation. The dead man has not yet been named."

Glossary

Bean-si (banshee) (n) – *An Irish female fairy who wails before a death in the family*

Face (n) – *Romantic encounter*

Fluke (n) – *Highly unlikely outcome*

Galloot (n) – *Silly person*

Pare (v) – *Split in sections using a spade*

Rassle (v) – *Wrestle*

Skiter (n) – *Derogatory term for a child*

Slagging (v) – *Verbal banter*